WAR OF THE BOOK

BY

JOSEPH A. WAILES

OUTLAW PRESS
RAWHIDE, TEXAS

COPYRIGHT © 2014
JOSEPH A. WAILES

ISBN 978-0-9916454-4-2
PRINTED AND BOUND IN
THE UNITED STATES OF AMERICA
ALL RIGHTS RESERVED

OUTLAW PRESS
2980 PHYLLIS LANE
RAWHIDE, TEXAS
75234-6425

THE WINNER OF THE HUMAN RACE

BY
JOSEPH A. WAILES

I_WHEN LIGHT BECAME A MAN

II_THE LONGEST NIGHT

III_ANCIENT DREAMS, NEWBORN VISIONS

IV_WAR OF THE BOOK

V_THE THIRD UNIVERSAL EVENT HORIZON

VI_HARVEST MOON

VII_TOO GOOD TO BE UNTRUE

BOOKS AVAILABLE AT OUTLAW PRESS

TABLE OF CONTENTS

0_FOREWORD..........................7
1_TOO WONDERFUL..................9
2_21 STEPS BEHIND JESUS..........13
3_THE EARTH-MAN SYSTEM.......17
4_TELL YOUR OWN STORY........26
5_RAPTORS............................36
6_SHEPHERD..........................41
7_NEED TO KNOW...................43
8_LONE RANGEL.....................50
9_YOUR GREATEST FEAR..........61
10_THE GOOD SAMERICANS.......70
11_JUDGE..............................80
12_WOLVES IN THE GARDEN......81
13_SHADOW OF DEATH.............90
14_OUT OF THE MAIN SEQUENCE............................101
15_TRUE...............................114
16_AUTOMATIC IDOLATRY......121
17_FIRSTBORN......................129
18_SEASONED WITH SALT.........145
19_TIRED ENOUGH TO SLEEP....171

20_THE MUSTARD PRINCIPLE....178
21_THE CORRECT PATTERN......184
22_THE FIRST RAINDROP..........191
23_THE FIRST NAVAL WAR.......199
24_BLESS GOD, AMERICA.........209
25_THE CONVERT....................210
26_IT'S A TRAP........................223
27_CARDIOMA.........................236
28_YOUR WAY.........................243
29_GULF OF FIRE.....................245
30_THE SANDAL STRAP............258
31_PROPHECY OF THE GOLDEN EAGLE....................................271
32_SIEGE MENTALITY...............278
33_TAKE AWAY THE STONE......295
34_CURRENTS OF JUSTICE.........311
35_HOW TO DECLARE SPIRITUAL BANKRUPTCY.........................321
36_WOLVES BEYOND THE GARDEN................................328
37_ABOUT THE AUTHOR'S LOBO......................................349
38_BACK-JACKET TEXT............351

FOREWORD

This is the fourth volume in this series. Each of the books corresponds to one of the four primary components of Creation, namely: energy, time, space, and matter. That is not the exclusive subject area, since other topics are also included.

You will notice recurring characters, themes, and concepts throughout the books. Some of the people and other creatures from book one are still active in book four. In the strictest sense of the concept, this can best be regarded as a loosely woven "quadrology", since a trilogy would only contain three books.

My function has been that of receiver antenna, through dreams, and so forth, and then transcriber, or maybe, describer, of the things which have been revealed to me. No two people have the same dreams, or visions. I know that I cannot personally see your own personal visions, or dreams. Neither can I show you mine, like letting you watch a movie of them. What I can do is to try to describe the things which I must, as clearly as possible. Just in case these ideas really were sent from God, maybe you should at least investigate them. Look and see, if you can perhaps find the ring of truth here, or, if not, show me where it can be disproved, from Scripture, only, not from somebody else's opinion. Scripture is authority, opinion is not.

TOO WONDERFUL

There be three things which are too wonderful for me, yea, four which I know not: the way of an eagle in the air, the way of a serpent upon a rock, the way of a ship in the midst of the sea, and the way of a man with a maid.

PROVERBS 30: 18, 19

Agur the Prophet, son of Jakeh, told this prophecy to King Ithiel and his brother, Ucal, long after the time of Solomon. The Lord Holy Spirit, through that prophet, shows us a deep look into the pattern and structure of both the Creator Himself, and also grants us a grand overview of the entire creation, salvation, and glorification process that Almighty God is still continuing, to this day.

In the first part, the three "things" correspond directly to the Father, Savior, and the Holy Spirit. The four things, second listed, correspond to the four primary structures of Creation, namely: energy, time, space, and matter.

The prophet also confesses that these "things" are too wonderful for him to be able to understand, even though he is aware that they do exist.

The next series of statements is a sequence of Spirit-given visions, and the result is the best practical description the prophet could write down. The way of an eagle in the air refers to Genesis, where "the Spirit of God was hovering above the waters". The way of a serpent upon a rock refers also to Genesis, where God cursed the serpent, and made him to go upon his belly upon the ground from then on, forever. The next vision is of a ship in the midst of the sea, as also occurred later in Genesis, and the ship was the Ark, and the captain was Noah.

The final mystery listed is the way of a man with a maid, and, although one might want to associate that with Adam and Eve, that does not follow the established format of the message, nor remain in keeping with its' positive tone. The whole thing is a snapshot of God's Creation, the fall, and God's judgment against the devil, and then God's saving grace to preserve mankind through Noah and the Ark. The much more likely association is that the way of a man with a maid actually is fulfilled in Matthew, and Luke, when Joseph obeys God's instructions to go ahead and stay with Mary, and the arriving Baby. Mary was still a maid, at that time, even though she was pregnant.

Joseph was one of the greatest men of faith in the whole Bible. Almost no other man would have shown the amazing patience, love, courage, and overwhelming FAITH that kept him moving in the paths of righteousness, as he obeyed God, and successfully protected and provided well for his new wife and Baby. The way Joseph did it was the only way any follower ever stays on track with the Lord.

He loved God, and he asked for directions, and, when God gave him directions, he followed, and he never gave up. That is why God the Father chose Joseph to become the Daddy of Jesus. God wanted the Baby to grow up knowing what a truly great father was like, and to learn from Joseph how to trust and obey the Heavenly Father in all things.

21 STEPS BEHIND JESUS

The other day, I drove over to the cemetery where my parents' bodies are resting. It was not a holiday, or any special day of remembrance. As is often the case, I just sometimes need to go there to pray, and remember the fine family I once was blessed to have known.

The location is at Restland Cemetery in Dallas, and the section is called the "Garden of the Good Shepherd". As I approached their gravesite, the sidewalk led toward a statue of Jesus, located about thirty feet away from my parents' spot. The statue stands facing the west, but I was drawing near from the east, so the back of the statue was the part I saw. On top of His shoulders, Jesus was carrying a little lamb.

I was immediately reminded of the part in Exodus where the Lord allows Moses to see Him, but only His back parts, since the glory and splendor of God's Face would have killed Moses, since no man can see God, and live.

I was also immediately reminded of the part in the Gospel of John where Jesus had met the disciples for breakfast, and as He walked along the beach with Peter, and Peter asked about what John would do, the good Lord told him not to worry about John, but for Peter just to concentrate upon following Jesus, and stick to that.

I stopped, and, as I looked at the back of the statue, my eyes were drawn to the very bottom edge of His robe, and I was reminded of the lady who said that if she could just touch the hem of His robe, she would be healed, and she was. I almost went over to the statue, to reach down, and touch the hem of His robe, but I did not. Instead, I stayed standing right where I was, about 21 steps behind the statue, since I knew it was just a statue, and not the Lord Himself.

Then, it occurred to me, that that makes a good illustration of where we all stand in this time. If each step corresponds to a century in time, then we are all about 21 steps behind Jesus. We know we cannot get ahead of Him, since He is the original pioneer, and the ultimate trailblazer. Nevertheless, we are commanded to follow Him, even if we cannot ever quite catch up. I know that my human legs are not long enough or strong enough to match the pace with God, so I remain a tag-along little brother of Jesus, always trying vainly to keep up.

That will have to suffice, for now. A servant cannot be greater than his Master. It is enough for us to be like Him. Even though I cannot quite ever catch up to Him, at least He left us a path we can follow. He was not kidding when He said He is the Way, the Truth, and the Life. Following His Way, in Truth, is the only chance any of us has to find Life. The Lord told us that the way to follow Him is to hear His commandments, and do them. Let us do that, and find Life everlasting.

THE EARTH-MAN SYSTEM

There appear to be many strange and fascinating parallels to be observed, in the structure of the planet Earth, and the individual human.

Of course, the first and most easily verified, by scientific methods, are the similarities in chemical composition, since our bodies are quite literally made out of the dust of our planet. The same precise atoms that each one of us wears around, as our physical flesh, are the same precise individual atoms that were long ago inside of earlier stars, until they exploded, scattering stardust all over the sky.

Eventually, over eons, enough of it clumped together again into huge masses of dust and gas, which were heated by compression, from gravity, until enough solid material, hydrogen gas, and heat were clumped together deep enough and hot enough to ignite a thermonuclear event, which was then sustained, by endless chain reaction explosions, as the new star blazed forth in the night!

Our star is thought to be a third generation star, because the heavy elements we find in our Solar System could only be formed in at least two passes through a supernova event, since that is the only known way in which the heavier elements will form, and that means there were at least two large stars in the Sun's family line ahead of him. Anyway, we are literally made of stardust: both our bodies, and our planet. That is not all.

The surface of the Earth is roughly 70% water, and 30% land. The composition of the human body is also about 70% water, and 30% solid matter.

The only part of the Earth with which we are able to directly interact is essentially the surface region itself, which corresponds to the skin, or outer appearance, of the human being. The deepest we have ever dived is about 7 miles, into the Marianna's Trench. The highest we have ever gone, without artificial aircraft, or spacecraft, is Mt. Everest, less than 6 miles tall.

In similar manner, we are usually only able to interact with most people which we encounter in a visual, or surface, manner. It is not really possible to see deep into a person, and to know what is really going on inside there, with the noted exception of x-rays, cat-scans, MRI's, and the like. Even more unfathomable may be the interior parts and workings of a person's heart and mind, especially since we all seem to practice keeping our cards close to our vest, in this gambling game called life, these days.

Another correlation is that with the Earth, it is often the deep, unseen, inner things that move and shift, and often, they can produce the greatest changes upon the surface. Earthquakes, tidal waves, and volcanic eruptions are among the more dramatic events, but a few months ago a careless oil company (from England) killed several people and millions of innocent sea creatures and birds, when they allowed a catastrophic well explosion in the Gulf of Mexico, and, once again, something far under the surface of the Earth began producing destruction upon the surface.

In like manner, it is always the hidden, inner things inside a person that move, and shift, and produce profound changes upon the surface. Such resulting changes could be in appearance, mannerisms, occupations, associations, affiliations, locations, destinations, or any other possible outward manifestation of change. Often, people are left completely mystified as to a possible motive for a certain change in a person's demeanor, or behavior, especially if the person has historically behaved in a very stable and predictable pattern. Sometimes insight is obtained, sometimes not.

As with the Earth, there is always much, much more to a person than meets the eye. The Lord warned us not to judge according to appearance, but to judge with righteous judgment. He also warned us not to answer a matter before we hear it. He also gave us an infallible litmus paper test to know (at least) the polarity of the person's heart, whether to do right, or to do evil. The Lord said that by their fruits we would know them. A good tree cannot bear bad fruit, nor can a bad tree bear good fruit. Know a person by their deeds, for their works bear them witness of what is really in their hearts.

The parallel structure is even extended to the relationship between the Sun and the Earth. The Sun would be just fine without the Earth, and maybe might not even notice, if Earth were to go wandering off into the night one day. Earth, without the Sun, is cold, dark, and dead, forever. As long as the Earth orbits the Sun, and stays close, faithfully, and continually, but still keeps a respectful distance, then the Earth will continue to survive and thrive just fine.

A very strong similarity exists in the relationship between God and man. As long as each one of us worships the good Lord, and stays with Him, we can receive life and hope and help from Him. Even so, we should always maintain a respectful distance, by being obedient to Him, and letting Him call all the shots, not us. His leadership is never the problem, but our "follower-ship" causes all the difficulties between us and Him. Remember, He never causes any difficulties between Him and us. He is trying to get along peacefully with us, and still manage to save our rebellious hides. It's not Him, it's us!

Where the Sun leads, Earth must obediently follow. Failure to do so would result in death.

Where the Lord leads, men must obediently follow. Failure to do so would result in death.

Another analogy is the Earth-Moon system. This is actually a double, or binary, planet system, and the Earth would be so much different without the Moon, that our physical environment would not support human life. Even though the Moon wears no green herself, she helps make it possible for the Earth to bear fruit, and good fruit, at that.

The Moon also orbits the Sun herself, but is dedicated, and forever bound, to be a partner with the Earth, and where the Earth leads, the Moon must follow.

This is much like the relationship between Adam and Eve, in many principles and aspects. It is unlikely that the good Lord arranged the massive structures of our Solar System in such a majestic demonstration of His sovereign plan (for the lives of Adam and Eve) without a lot of thought and careful planning. Only God could use the Sun and planets to write His Holy message, concerning living relationships, between God, man, and woman. This shows what His great design for us has always been, when He designed and built the Solar System.

Another illustration was also given to us by the good Lord. He showed us that, as each of the planets travels in its' own special path around the Sun, every single one of them relates to the Sun, first, and most. He's the Big Boss. Not one of the single individual planets is ever expected, or even actually permitted, to criticize another planet's orbital behavior.

Jesus told Peter not to worry about what He had planned for John, but to focus upon Peter's own assignments from then on. Maybe we, as 21st Century Christians, should worry a little less about how every one else is following, or not following, the good Lord, and focus more upon being careful, every day, to follow Him better ourselves!

TELL YOUR OWN STORY

Ever since he had asked the question, some inner compass had always continually and accurately given the answer. It was immediately after he had washed the saltwater out of his eyes and beard, that he had blinked in the bright sunlight, looked straight up overhead into a limitless blue sky, and whispered, "Whatever you want, Lord! Which way is Nineveh?" The Lord had instantly answered, and the internal compass needle never wavered, or stopped working, day or night, though he still could sleep and rest at night along his road.

He had a long journey over land, and the Lord had instructed him to walk, not ride, but to rest frequently, and eat and drink extra rations to re-build his strength. After all, three days in the absolute dark, up to his waist in cold water, with nothing to eat (and only foul, fish-stinking water inside the fish with him, and deadly salt water from the sea, at that) had left him a lot more weakened, and more badly shaken than he ever would have expected.

The good Lord had opened his eyes to see into the spiritual zone, just as he had washed the salt crystals out of his eyes. Now, as he walked along the road, he could clearly see the guardian angel personally assigned to him. The angel spoke rarely, except to warn him of approaching danger, and the whole time, the angel's expression remained calmly focused, with a slight hint of a smile in a face that was both stunningly beautiful, and at the same time terrifying enough to make a man's hands start shaking, and his mouth go dry with fear. This man had realized instinctively that he did not want to anger the good angel, or stare directly into his eyes. Even if the war-angel was friendly enough, and extremely comforting to have along for the journey, the man was exceedingly glad that the angel was on his side. It made sleeping in the open in the mild weather a safe and affordable way to rest at night. The man had noticed that even the mosquitoes and ants would not come anywhere near him or the angel, and he never got even a flea bite during the journey.

As the man walked, and grew stronger, he continually was in prayer and communion with the good Lord. He prayed out loud, usually, since no one else was around but the Lord, and the angel, to hear. Sometimes, he sang psalms in rhythm to his marching steps.

He was confused about what he would tell the people of Nineveh. In the future, 2,600 years later, the people would be known as the Kurds, and the main city would then be called Mosul. That was not his concern. He did not fear for his own safety, any longer, just as long as he did not end up in that damn fish's belly again. Besides, even if no one else could see the mighty angel, he was still there. He was just at a loss as to what could convince people of the truth, whose entire belief system included frequent human sacrifices, always of the people they had captured from other countries, or occasionally, people dumb enough to offend their own king.

The Lord told him to warn them that in another 40 days, a rapidly growing, nearby country, named Assyria, was going to be headed toward Nineveh, to utterly crush and enslave it forever. The Lord was no particular fan of Assyria, but it was just slightly less deplorable than Nineveh. This would be the only chance that the good Lord was going to send to Nineveh, to repent of their evil, and begin to live correctly before Him, the Judge of the whole world. If they heard, and changed, and stayed changed, God promised He would spare them, but if not, they would be obliterated, and the name of their nation forgotten forever.

The man agreed instantly to do precisely that, but still was not sure what more he should tell them. The Lord told him to tell them about his own misadventures, that had landed him in the fish's belly, but to also include how the good Lord had shown mercy to him, when he repented, and then had spared his life and restored him to strength, and even graciously given him back his mission to complete, including sending the courage and wisdom to finish it right.

The man smiled, thanked the good Lord, and rolled over to fall asleep, while his friend the angel sat over by the little campfire, keeping it well tended all night.

The next day, they began to see many more people, as they entered the outer districts of the huge city. Nineveh was over thirty miles in diameter, and had, at that time, about an eighth of a million people living there. Some people began to speak to him, but before they could say anything more than "Hey!" he would drown them out with a commanding roar to "REPENT, SINNER!!!" That would instantly shut them up. Then, as they blinked their eyes in confusion and uncertainty, he would begin to tell them precisely the things the Lord had instructed him to say. He never stopped walking, or talking, for three days and nights, as he slowly neared the central region, where the king's palace was located. Several times along the way, official guards of the city tried to stop him, or block his path, but he kept right on walking, not even looking at them, preaching loudly with every step, the same message, over and over. The second group of guards had actually been stupid enough to fire a few arrows at him, but the arrows spun in mid-air at the halfway point to him, and then returned to kill their own archers. After that, no one wanted to dare even throw an apple core at him. They just kept trying to block the street in front of him, and the unseen angel just pushed the horses and men out of the way, every time, as though they were made of cardboard. They could not stop the prophet, or shut him up, since the Lord had amplified his voice to almost deafening decibel levels, and it was like listening to a rock concert ordering people to "REPENT!!!"

Finally he reached the palace gate. It was locked tight, with many steel bars and locks, and he looked at it for a minute, and then, to the gate itself, shouted "REPENT, SINNER!!!"

The gate exploded inwards as though hit by a tank round. After the dust cleared a bit, and debris stopped falling out of the air, he walked into the palace, and straight up to the king, seated upon his fancy throne. The terrified king's face was almost white with fear, and he even was trembling at the sight of this strange visitor. He began to shout orders to his guards to drop their weapons at once. As the guards were laying down their swords and spears, and bows, the king threw his crown down on the throne, as he jumped up, and ran over to Jonah, and fell to his knees before the prophet, asking for God to have mercy upon himself, and all of his people, and their city. He confessed the sin of Nineveh, and himself, and ordered for every one, man and beast, to be covered in sackcloth, and to fast from food and water, and to cry out in prayer to Almighty God, to have mercy, and for every one to turn away from their violence, and wickedness.

As the king, and the rest of his court, sat, stunned, silent, and utterly beaten, the prophet Jonah continued to tell them of the wonders wrought by the Holy God of Israel, Who is Lord of Heaven and Earth, and made all things in them, including man. He also obediently told them how he had gone from a rich man in Jerusalem, as a highly paid advisor to his own Hebrew king, to a disobedient prophet, and that God decided that he should spend a little quality time alone, in the depths of the dark sea, breathing rotten air inside a fish's belly. He also told them how he had confessed his own sin of rebellion before God, and promised to never disobey again, if given a second chance. Then he told them of the wonderful miracle, of the Lord suddenly being there inside the fish with him, and telling him that he was forgiven, and now would he continue with the mission, please? That was an offer no one could refuse, and Jonah had gratefully accepted.

    Jonah continued preaching and teaching for about six weeks, and the whole city came to listen, and repent, and pray, and commit their lives to abandon their old ways, and walk in new, righteous ways. They even began to study the Hebrew scripture, and to study the ways of Israel, and they altogether discontinued human sacrifice. Jonah was good, indeed, but he had a fiery temper, too, and he became very angry when the men of Nineveh began to worship as Hebrews did, but none of them would get circumcised. Jonah left the city in a huff, and went out and sat fuming under a shady tree. God asked him why he was so steamed, and then reminded him that this was supposed to be a mission of mercy, and it was not good form for Jonah to get all bent out of shape over a technicality. Jonah thought it over for a minute, remembering that the good Lord had just recently forgiven him, and shown him mercy, too. Jonah bowed his head, and shook it in self-dismissal.

"Oh, of course, You're right, Lord! Thank You for reminding me. Sorry that I forgot so soon. I guess we're done here. Now, which way is Jerusalem?"

RAPTORS

This last year has been marked by some very unusual sights. Although, by the generous and faithful grace of our good Lord, I still am allowed to dwell in the same home where I was planted, at the age of five years, I have seen some strange, never-before-seen displays. (That doesn't mean other folks have never seen those sights, or greater still, just that I never saw them here, in my 53 years at this same blessed home.)

One example that I recall was a huge, slow-motion massive snow event, the largest and most impressive we ever had in Dallas. There was also the giant silver-leaf maple tree in our front yard, which was planted there about a week before we moved into our new home, on April 1, 1957. After all these decades enduring storms, winters, merciless summers, bugs, and birds carving nests into it, it has finally begun to pass away. It saddens my heart, as though I have lost another dear family member. It was the only thing, except for the Lord, and me, that has been here the entire time, since 1957. (Well, I guess my guardian angel has been here, too, and has proven his skill in protecting me many, many times.)

    Yesterday evening, a little while before sundown, I noticed outside the window a busy swarm of bugs, darting and zipping every which way, at very high speeds. There was something very odd about their manner of flight, and I was led, by curiosity, outside, for a closer look. As one zipped close by my face I could understand instantly. They were the helicopters of the insect world, namely, dragonflies! With their four main wings, which rotate this way and that, they can hover, fly backward, accelerate like a shot, and turn in mid-flight on a dime! I saw maybe 100 or more of them, each one busy chasing down and snagging mouthful after mouthful of their favorite snack, mosquitoes. They were all moving at remarkable speed, yet never did have a collision with each other. They all worked individually, but all together, at the same task, which was to eat every single mosquito in my front yard! I smiled, and looking up, and thanked our good Lord for His extra help. The evening before, I had been out in the yard for about two minutes, and was awarded many bites on my legs. I had actually cursed the mosquitoes to die suddenly, but then forgotten about it.

As I watched them working tirelessly, and very effectively, I noticed that the mosquitoes were invisible to me, if more than three feet away, but the mighty dragonflies saw and ate every one. When I went out earlier this evening, nothing was left there to bite me.

I know some people might say it was just coincidence, but then again, what do they know, anyway? I am not responsible if they cannot believe the plain evidence. We do indeed have a great and loving God, One that cares even about a bunch of vampire mosquitoes, and does not want them to chew on His little friend, me.

The dragonflies had concentrated their efforts around the side of the front yard where the old tree still fights to survive. It made me think how the Lord sends His good angels to hunt down and kill or drive away the deadly, harassing enemies we cannot see with our natural eyes. This old tree is still fighting to survive, too. It is of great encouragement to know that there are friendly hunters patrolling the zone around me, killing or driving away things that I cannot even see.

Maybe the old tree will make it, maybe not. It had a great, long life, and added much beauty and joy to our lives here. If it can survive, and grow strong again, I will rejoice. If not, I will remember it with joy, and always be thankful that I knew it, and shared my lifetime here with it.

One thing that sticks with me, though, is this: the description of how the good Lord sends out His angels at the time of Judgment, and how they cover the whole world, rounding up every wicked creature, and forcefully removing them from the Earth, reminds me a lot of what I saw the dragonflies doing. None of those mosquitoes escaped, or could fight back, and none of the evil creatures will be able to do so, either!

SHEPHERD

sheep sheep sheep sheep sheep sheep
sheep sheep sheep sheep sheep sheep
sheep sheep sheep sheep sheep sheep
sheep sheep sheep sheep sheep sheep
sheep sheep sheep sheep sheep sheep
sheep sheep sheep sheep sheep sheep
sheep sheep sheep sheep sheep sheep
sheep sheep sheep sheep sheep sheep
sheep sheep sheep sheep sheep sheep
sheep sheep sheep sheep sheep sheep
sheep sheep sheep sheep sheep sheep
sheep sheep sheep sheep sheep sheep
sheep sheep sheep sheep sheep sheep
sheep sheep sheep sheep sheep sheep
sheep sheep sheep sheep sheep sheep
sheep sheep sheep sheep sheep sheep
sheep sheep sheep sheep sheep sheep
sheep sheep sheep sheep sheep sheep

sheep sheep sheep sheep sheep sheep
sheep sheep sheep sheep sheep sheep
sheep sheep sheep sheep sheep sheep
sheep sheep sheep sheep sheep sheep
sheep sheep sheep sheep sheep sheep
sheep sheep sheep sheep sheep sheep

(Continued to Infinity: Confirmed for Eternity)

NEED TO KNOW

One of the concepts with which I became familiar during my military service was a thing called "need to know". This refers to classified information, items of knowledge categorized variously as confidential, secret, and top secret. Such things could include weapons systems, troop deployments, strength of forces in the field, planned movement or timing strategies, and the whole complex mess of details our side does not want the other side to find out. The method applied, to reduce accidental spillage of classified information, is to restrict just how many people, and precisely which people, are allowed to even know those items to start. If a person cleaning the galley on a Navy ship does not ever work on torpedoes, then he has no requirement to learn all about torpedoes. Therefore, the person does not have a "need to know" anything at all about torpedoes, except to stay away from them.

This arrangement appears effective, and is rigorously enforced. Depending upon the details and severity of any willful infraction, the offender could be charged with treason, and, in time of war, executed.

Notice how a parallel is revealed in the final few chapters of Job, the first-written book of the Bible. The Lord challenges Job about some of the amazing mysteries of nature, and the unknown aspects of His glorious creation. Job cannot answer God, except to admit that he is, just like all of us, only an animated mud-ball, and should not even dare to speak to God at all, except to thank Him, and to apologize for being a failure as a human being, just like all the rest of us, except for Jesus Christ. We were created in God's image, to be like Him, and He does not ever sin. Except for Jesus Christ, all of us do sin.

A lot of people wonder what it was that Job did to make God mad at him. That was the same thing that puzzled Job. Job was brilliant, and quick to learn, and honest, and humble, and he truly loved God with all of his whole heart. Even when things were absolutely ruined and destroyed, Job still loved God, and would not falsely charge the good Lord with any wrongdoing. Job knew already that God does not do anything wrong, and He never makes any mistakes at all.

Job knew that he loved the Lord, and he knew that God is never wrong. Job's conclusion was that he must have done something very wrong, indeed, to have the destruction of his entire life forced upon him. His only mistake was that he thought that God owed him an explanation as to the reason why the Lord had allowed such catastrophes to occur, since He could have prevented it all, or at least softened the blow a bit.

After the "nature quiz" which Job could in no way answer, the point was clear. No one ever has any right to demand answers from God. On the contrary, it is God Who will demand answers from each of us.

Job confessed his impertinence, and asked forgiveness, for himself, and his own sinful, lying friends. Job forgave his friends their hurtfulness unto him, during his affliction. Then the Lord immediately forgave them all, since He said He would listen to Job's prayer, since Job was humble, and honest. He restored Job to more than double his former wealth and power. Many centuries later, at least a thousand years, a far-downstream blood-line descendent of Job, named Abraham, would be called out by God to found a new nation of His own chosen people. All because Job humbly and honestly obeyed God in everything he was commanded. He did it from the heart, because he loved the good Lord.

I must admit that I often face the same dilemma Job encountered. I know that I love the good Lord, and I try very hard to obey Him, in spirit and truth, but my life, although wonderfully blessed in numerous ways, still has its' own share of pain and sorrow (who doesn't?). After a long time wrestling with a medical, or financial, or emotional difficulty, it is very easy to become discouraged, when it seems as though your prayers are being ignored. It becomes a short step of "logic" to conclude that one's life must be displeasing to the good Lord, and who but the Lord Himself could even properly evaluate whether any individual's life is more pleasing or displeasing unto the One Who judges us. No one can see into the heart of a person as clearly as the Lord, including the person himself. The one Person with which you will never get away with a lie is the good Lord, but the easiest person in the world to convince of a lie is yourself. That is why it is impossible for the natural man to understand the things of God. With God's Word, and the Holy Spirit, a reborn person will begin to clearly perceive the issues of the Gospel, and the Kingdom of Heaven, but a worldly person cannot.

In military terms, God told Job, very gently, that Job did not have a "need to know" why all the tragedy and loss had happened to his life. Even though this is literally true, it is a hard, bitter pill to swallow. Job accepted it humbly, honestly, and graciously, and followed God's instructions to the letter, after that. That is one of the main reasons why God includes Job in the all-time greats list among men, also naming Noah and Daniel. All of them were extraordinarily patient men, and each of them loved the Lord more than his own life. All of them stuck tight with the Lord, running to Him, instead of from Him, whenever things got tough. Mighty men, indeed!

I do wrestle with the same issues, but I am not as tough as those greats. I have to ask the good Lord to even help me keep on trying, if that is what He wants me to do. Maybe that is the precise condition and attitude He requires for me, for now. Okay.

I still love Him. I still want to stay with Him forever. I still do not understand it all. I first told Him those things when I was eight years old, and I still mean them now, fifty years later. I wonder just how long before He starts the Jubilee?

I suppose, for now, I have no "need to know". Instead, I now have a "need to trust".

LONE RANGEL

Precisely one week after the events which led me to write the story "Raptors", a strange follow-up event occurred. The first story was about several dragonflies clearing my whole front yard of nasty mosquitoes for me. The next evening, they did not return, since they had completed their rescue mission the evening prior.

The parallel vision of dragonflies sent by the good Lord to clear my home of evil mosquitoes, and good angels sent by the good Lord to clear and defend my home and me from evil spirits, was a correlation too obvious to miss. The good Lord also promised that He will send all of the good angels to destroy all the evil out of the world when the proper time arrives.

After I saw this, I wrote the first story, and thought no more about it, until seven days later, at the same time of late afternoon, a little before sunset, when I noticed a single dragonfly patrolling the front yard, and hunting and killing new mosquitoes that had hatched during the week. A parallel was revealed unto me in this event.

When the need had been extreme, the good Lord had sent much help to overcome the enemy. When the same need arose again, a week later, the Lord sent as much help as needed, right then, to maintain the environment clear and free of evil. This is the same thing we know, from His Word, that He does for each one of us who love and follow Him.

We know that each one of us is assigned a particular individual protector. As the Holy Spirit guards our hearts, minds, and spirits, which are re-born of Him, the good angels are given charge over our physical protection. There are more instances, in my own life, of a sudden rescue from severe bodily harm or death than I can even list or remember, though I do know they have been occurring all of my life, and I am sure each believer can also share the same experiences. Often, I realize there are many times in which the danger is quietly averted, and the protection is maintained, achieved so effectively, smoothly, and quickly, that we are not even aware that a danger existed.

When I recall all of those moments of mercy and grace, I am greatly encouraged to continue on in my efforts to glorify our good Lord. Indeed, since the Lord is on our side, all we need to retain in focus is that we remain in agreement with the Lord. "There is no wisdom, understanding, or counsel against the Lord."

It might have been that I would not have ever been carried to term, and actually born into this world. A lot can happen in nine months. When I was a baby, something happened inside my intestines, and I nearly died. The damage from that infant sickness has never fully healed, and has plagued me all my life, but it did not kill me.

When I was six years old, I was riding my little bicycle across a wide field, which we used for our baseball games. There was a path worn through the field, where we all rode our bikes to get to the shopping center on the other side. An older, but much more stupid boy came roaring up the little path behind me, riding a mini-bike. I knew already, even at six, that when a faster vehicle approaches from behind, one is supposed to pull over to the right, and let the faster traffic pass, safely. I did what I had been taught. The idiot on the mini bike was an untrained loser, and also decided to go to the right, to try an unsafe pass. A second later, I was hurled up into the air! As the jerk and his machine smashed into the back of my bike, and I did a complete mid-air back flip. I landed safely on my butt, stunned, but alive, and not crippled. I made it on home, with only some scratches and a dinged-up back fender.

Very many times in my life, death threatened me, with all manner of deadly attempts, ranging from car accidents, motorcycle wrecks, exploding machinery, like a clutch in my car, all the way to fists, boots, dog teeth, electrocution, asphyxiation, drowning, poisoning, and so forth. Once, during an initiation in boy scouts, at Camp Constantine, I was accidentally set on fire by some of my fellow scouts!

There were times when people pointed loaded guns at me, and only a few of them were police. Most of them were crazy criminals, and that description could well apply to some of the more deranged cops, too. What some of them did and said was obviously evil. Hey, cops are people, too, and some of them readily lie and falsify information to make their actions look better. A badge does not automatically make a person righteous.

My Dad was a police Detective in Birmingham, Alabama, after World War II. My Dad was a very good policeman. Dad resigned, after he and Mom had enough money saved, to buy the laundry which they rebuilt, and ran, until 1953, when they sold it, and moved us to Texas to be closer to Mom's side of the family.

There were many, many times also in the lives of both of my parents where serious injury, or death, was averted in the last split-second. Dad was a Navy Commander, and was the Executive Officer of the Leyte Island Strike Force, including about 150 PT boats and their men. He was the chief strategist for the Pacific PT boat actions in World War II, and was extremely effective in his work. Before he was promoted to Executive Officer, he spent a lot of months out in battle, as skipper of his own PT boat, and squadron leader for other boats with them. One night, on a moonlit patrol along the coast, an American pilot, with more gung-ho than good sense, decided that my Dad's boat was Japanese, and tried to bomb them out of the water. The dangerous American pilot only broke off the attack when my Dad had all of the boats with him open up with their 50 calibers, since, even though they knew the plane was American, it was either take the plane out, or let the idiot kill them all. The plane broke off the attack, with no casualties. When my Dad and his men returned to base the next morning, the Commanding Officer called my Dad into his office, and began to chew him out for firing upon an American plane, until my Dad explained that the jerk was trying to kill them all first. After confirmation of the truth my Dad told, the pilot was busted, and never flew again, after his court-martial. My Dad was soon promoted, and again and again, he was decorated, and promoted, and for the last three years of the war, was the effective leader of the PT boat war in the Pacific.

The point is this. Even though a crazy jerk in a plane almost murdered my Dad one night, none of the many bombs they dropped ever hit any of them. Also, the fool was broken, justly, and my Dad was promoted, justly. The angels protected Dad in battle, and the good Lord exonerated him, and promoted him instead.

When my Mom was in school, at Union Theological Seminary in Richmond, Virginia, she was working on her Master's degree in theology. During the summers, she and other students did not just go home for the summer, they were sent out into the world for a few weeks, to preach the gospel. Mom was sent into Appalachia, and every Sunday, she went across the river to a small open-air chapel in the woods, where all the local folks could come to worship, and hear her speak. Since she had to be there early, she would arrive at the river bank right at sunrise, say a prayer, and climb, with tremendous courage, into the little row boat she had to use to get across. The river was dangerous, and she was alone, except for the good Lord, and the good angels. She trusted the Lord, and rowed herself across the raging river, many times. Mom was not just afraid of getting a little splashed. She could not swim. Every time she got into the boat, she was risking her life, just to go preach. I do not know just how many close calls with death she fought, but I know her faith and courage were mighty, and so were the Lord and the good angels.

There was the time a crazy former employee from the laundry came into the lunch diner where they all ate lunch, and tried to kill my Mom with a butcher knife. The good angels got her up and moving fast enough so that she made it out of the diner, and began running down the sidewalk. Some kid had left his bike laying on the sidewalk, and my Mom, with either an extra burst of adrenaline, or maybe a hand from her angel, managed to jump clear over the bike, and keep running for her life, but the beast chasing her tripped and fell, and she escaped.

So, if you personally do not think we each have guardian angels protecting us, you are mistaken. My own life, and the lives of my parents, are proof, again and again, that we are indeed protected, extremely well. The fact that I am still alive and well enough to sit here at the keyboard, and write this story today is living proof. If either of my parents had been taken out, I would not be here, or, if I had been taken out, same result.

Therefore, a single dragonfly hunting down mosquitoes in my front yard does indeed speak to my spirit about guardian angels. It is very helpful to know that there is always at least one of them around, keeping watch over each one of us who loves the Lord, according to His purpose.

YOUR GREATEST FEAR

Human beings have fears. Part of that may be the fact that a creature with a vulnerable, breakable body is often required to use caution in any physical activity that involves risk of injury. Part of that may be the emotional uncertainty produced, because an inherent limitation is common to all men, namely, the inability to clearly perceive the details of future events. The most powerful reason that we have fear is that we are born as fallen creatures, already, at birth, into a fallen world, right from the second of our arrival.

In the Garden of Eden, Adam spoke directly, face to Face, with Almighty God, and yet the human, Adam, felt no fear. That was because he was still righteous, and had nothing at all to fear from God.

Right after Adam had listened to his wife, instead of the Lord, and had tasted the apple also, he was then found hiding from God, and admitted that he was now afraid of God. Adam knew he had disobeyed God, and now he had something indeed to fear, even death. God is absolute King. For anyone to rebel against Him is death, for the offender.

Note how bravely Adam tried to pass the blame on to his beloved wife. Note how men and women have been doing that to each other ever since.

Now, some humans (like you and me) that were not there, and did not live out those real-world events at the dawn of time, might think we could have done better, and not eaten the damn apple. Do not lie to yourself. Each one of us does plenty of sin every single day of our lives in this world, whether we even notice it, or not.

Anyway, Adam now had fear, and he did not hesitate to instantly junk his relationship with Eve, because his greatest fear was God. The way that Adam, the first human man to ever feel fear, dealt with his fear, was to first, respond exclusively to his greatest fear, disregarding all else, and second, employ a tactic to draw fire away from himself, to a target of less importance to him than his own skin. Fortunately, trying to bluff or smokescreen God never works. Unfortunately, all of us have been doing the same sort of behavior pattern ever since, when faced with our own greatest fear.

Even though this is not a pleasant topic, nor a very flattering look at humanity, still, it is easier to deal with an enemy when you rip the mask off of it. The outward behavior is labeled as everything from just good, old fashioned common sense, to extreme prudence, or over cautiousness. "You can never be too careful!"

Now, to rip off that mask, it amounts to a degree of cowardice we inherited from birth into a fallen world, from fallen parents. Sorry, to have to be the one to tell you.

In a nutshell, the practical mechanism that dictates a lot of our actions, plans, dreams, projects, and other busy pursuits, is simply fear. What ever thing we fear the most, it is that most-feared thing which we will make all possible effort to avoid.

That is why the good Lord Jesus told us all that we should fear Him, in His role as Judge of the whole world. He warned us to fear the One Who, after He killed, had power to cast into the Lake of Fire, where both soul (heart and mind) and body would be destroyed. That description only can ever apply to the good Lord Jesus, and no one else. If we fear offending Him, then we will live lives less offensive unto Him.

The only other human man, that felt no fear, was Jesus. Adam felt fear after he sinned, but Jesus never sinned. Perfect love casts out fear, and Jesus is perfect love. In the Gospels we are told that Jesus was depressed, and that he was so stressed out about His upcoming ordeal, that he wished He already had it over. He was so very stressed out during His prayers that he became drenched with sweat, not blood. His blood flowed later the next day.

The thing He warned His followers about, right before His arrest, was to pray, to not enter into temptation. Whoever commits sin is a slave of sin, and He wanted His followers to stay free, since He was about to go endure unimaginable agony and death to win our freedom. He wants for us to fear God in our hearts, so we do not want to sin, and He wants us to flee from temptation, since only Jesus was ever strong enough to take temptation on hand to hand, and whip it. No one but Jesus can do that.

In the Revelation of Jesus to His follower, John, we are told that the good Lord will wipe every tear from our eyes, and that no one will make us afraid, anymore. That is certainly in complete keeping with all of His other goodness unto us, but it is something more, too. We are being transformed into the precise likeness of Jesus, as we live our lives loving Him. Jesus does not cry any more, now that His mission is complete, and we also will not cry anymore when our missions are complete. When it comes to fear, Jesus never was afraid, and someday, none of us will be afraid any longer, either. So, when you fight depression, remember that our good Lord also fought it, and won, and since He never sinned, depression is not a sin, but a sinful world does depress God's people. Keep fighting depression, with deliberate hope in Jesus.

When you are fighting stress, remember that our good Lord also fought stress, and beat it. Again, since He never sinned, stress is not a sin, but it does wear you out, and distracts you from giving your best performance. Keep on fighting stress, by deliberately trusting in Jesus. Ask Him to help, too.

When you are fighting pain, remember that our good lord Jesus also fought pain, and beat it magnificently. Again, since He never sinned, it is not a sin to feel pain. Keep on fighting pain by trusting in Jesus, asking Him to help, and remember that someday, we also, as with Him, will feel no more pain.

It is my humble and sincere prayer, that some of these observations will benefit my brothers and sisters in Jesus. I also have a lot of trouble fighting stress, depression, and pain. I would have been overcome, or given up, long ago, if our good Lord had not given me enough strength to keep going. He has kept me in the game this long, so I guess He will keep me in the game as long as He sees fit, whether I think I can take it any longer or not. Very well, I am willing to let God be God, since I am not.

When you are fighting fear, remember that our good Lord Jesus never was afraid of anybody, or anything. Ask Him to give you a little bit more of His courage, to get you through, and calm you down. He does not mind, and He has always helped me when I asked Him for courage. Otherwise, I would have been a shaking wreck many times. He has plenty of courage to share, and He is listening to hear our requests. Pray, if you are wise, to be granted courage before the fight, because things happen fast in a fight, and you may need courage the second it starts, and not have time to ask for it then. Also, please pray for me to be brave, since I sometimes still have to fight fear, too. I also try to choose the things which I will allow myself to fear. I would rather fear the good Lord, than the bad devil. At least with the good Lord, there is some possibility for mercy.

Also, the Lord can deliver you from the devil, but no one can deliver you from God, if He is after you. You go right ahead, and just try to out run Him. You will have better results running to Him, than away from Him.

THE GOOD SAMERICANS

What ever happened to the Samaritans? After the Assyrian army conquered the Northern Kingdom and carried most of the people away, all of the ten Northern tribes were forcibly scattered to the far corners of the world. In modern times, we can trace some of their pathways. The evacuation began even before the total collapse of the North had been finalized, as many people saw and understood that their nation was indeed under condemnation, and that God had judged them to be in dire need of destruction. The good Lord of Israel had been very patient with them, but finally had been forced to correct their idolatries and blasphemies, if He was ever to be able to save their future descendents.

We know that they ended up, over the next few centuries, as far removed as China, Africa, Asia Minor, Europe, even as far north as the Scandinavian lands, and Russia, and, of course, the British Islands. As even more centuries of time passed, later descendents crossed oceans, to establish new communities and nations, all over the entire Earth, wherever men could live. No other group of people has ever been scattered so very far, from a single original nation.

As the memories of their ancestry faded over time, the people forgot that they were ever even a part of Israel, and could not have traced their connections to ancient Samaria without the use of modern DNA techniques. If it had not been for the Holy Spirit causing those long-lost people to become born again, and to be reconciled into the Kingdom of Heaven, through the body and the blood of the Lord Jesus, they would have remained cut off from hope forever. God had promised something wonderful to His servant Abraham, and God is faithful to keep His promises, even over centuries of time, and even in far-flung lands. The promise was that the good Lord would carefully watch over the scattered remnants of Israel, and would preserve them, until a future time, when He would call each of His estranged prodigal children home again to Him. He has faithfully already done this, since every believer in Jesus Christ has become fully reconciled through Christ.

So, what common points can we observe today, between ancient Samaritans, and modern Americans? Well, each group of folks believed in the God of Israel. Each group also had radical differences of opinion between themselves and the remaining tribes, Judah and Benjamin. Did anyone else notice that the two remaining tribes were the tribe of inheritance, Judah, and the tribe of the last-born child of Jacob, Benjamin? Certainly this was not an accidental arrangement by our good Lord. Perhaps He is signaling unto us that the inheritance will still be granted, even unto the last-born, and the last-re-born, of all of the children of Israel. This will still be graciously achieved by the good Lord, even if the descendents do not fully realize from just whom they themselves are descended. Even if the people have forgotten their past heritage, God has not forgotten, and He will still perform His mercy.

Another aspect of this scattering was that Hebrew people became embedded within every nation and culture upon Earth. Yes, there are some modern exceptions, such as the head-hunters of Borneo, but the scattering is still continuing, even this day, and ultimately, Israel will be scattered to every nation. Their arrival may be presented as Christian missionaries, but they are still the spiritual, and, in most cases, also the physical, descendents of Abraham, Isaac, and Jacob. In this work, the good Lord has fulfilled His command for us to go, be fruitful, and to multiply, filling the Earth with His glory, and His people. Also, this is another kept promise, that in Israel, all the nations of the Earth would be blessed. Also, the good Lord told us that He would not return until the Gospel had been preached in all the Earth. The people who are doing that are indeed the descendents of Abraham, Isaac, and Jacob. In the long run, the children of Abraham will become uncountable in number.

So, do the modern Americans do the works of ancient Israel, or not? Well, we do preach the truth about God, and the Kingdom of Heaven, unto the whole world. This indeed was something that ancient Israel also did, though they had not yet met the King of Kings in Person.

Also, we do indeed try to bless and help those in the heathen nations, such as Pakistan, where the people curse us, and try to kill us, but scream like brats for emergency help, whenever the big river floods them out. So, we try to forgive, and turn the other cheek, and help the ingrates, anyway, because the good Lord told us to do so. They demand our help, but will not give us even a minimum of respect. God has the same precise problem with every human, except for Jesus.

If you wish to consider the more scientific blessings directly from Israel, we can start with the modern cell phone. It was developed in Israel. Also from Hebrews came RFID microchips, as well as high-tech advances in agriculture, even to the point that today, Israel is the breadbasket for much of the world. In Europe, and most of the Mid East, if you want fresh, good quality fruit, you must purchase it from Israel. We do not know all of the military high-tech weapons and advances Israel has achieved, unless they choose to share them with us. We know of one device, in which a sensor can detect explosives in a person's backpack, over a half mile away, and then fire an unseen high frequency laser into the pack, and detonate it safely before the insane terrorist ever reaches his objective. Every time you have heard in the news, at least in the last two years, that a terrorist "accidentally" blew himself up, in Israel, rest assured, it was not an accident, at all. In medical technology, Israel has pioneered advances in minimally invasive surgical methods, which are now being accepted and adopted in the United States, and other nations.

When it comes to hand-to-hand combat, the Krav Maga defense system, developed and refined by Israel, is proven to be the most effective of the whole world's fighting systems. It is also the easiest to learn, being structured upon a person's instinctive response to threat.

When it comes to diplomacy, no other nation has ever put the rest of the world through their paces at the bargaining table more, or more extensively, than

Israel. The major problem for Israel, at the moment, in that arena, is that their primary ally, the United States, has, again and again, sold them up the river for the sake of convenience, or a better oil deal with the Arabs. Be very cautious, great and mighty men and women of the United States government. Remember, God is watching, and listening, and you had better stop trying to tell Israel how to settle and build in its' own God-granted lands (see Genesis).

Never forget God's declared promise, and dire threat, concerning how we treat Israel. Those who bless Israel, God Himself will bless. Those who curse Israel, God Himself will curse. He means it.

The split between Samaria and Israel goes all the way back to David's grandson. It was less than a century later that the Northern tribes broke away, and distanced themselves from Israel proper. It was only a few decades later that the

Assyrian army arrived, and carried away, physically, all of the descendents of the renegade Samaritans.

In that respect, also, America has followed the trend of Samaria, and set itself apart from Israel, way too much. All of our good deeds, and all of our good works, will still not be able to overpower the promise of God. If we are against Israel, then God is against us. If only the deluded presidents and state department folks would wake up, and start to actually help Israel, instead of trying to rule over it! Maybe our economy would improve, and maybe our disasters, like Katrina, and the idiots from BP spilling poison all over the Gulf, and lying every day about it, might finally be halted. If we confess our sins, and forsake them, God will restore us. If we continue hard headed and proud hearted, our good Lord will discipline us, even to the point of destruction, if needed.

There is one bright note, however. The folks of the village of Sychar, in Samaria, at Jacob's well, heard, believed, and accepted the good Lord Jesus when He went and spoke to them. In that case, they far outshone their Israeli cousins to the south. We are similar unto Samaria in that way, also. To this day, most Jews do not accept the true identity of Jesus Christ of Nazareth as the Holy Begotten Son of God. Jesus is also the Son of Man, as described in the prophecies. When, sometime in the future, Israel has begun to accept their rightful King, Jesus, the good Lord will begin to fulfill yet another of His mighty promises. He will begin to gather together all of the far-scattered children of light, so there will be One Shepherd, and His sheep, from many different places, will be gathered together into the Shepherd's sheepfold!

JOSEPH A. WAILES

JUDGE

sheep sheep sheep   goat goat goat
sheep sheep sheep   goat goat goat
sheep sheep sheep   goat goat goat
sheep sheep sheep   goat goat goat
sheep sheep sheep   goat goat goat
sheep sheep sheep   goat goat goat
sheep sheep sheep   goat goat goat
sheep sheep sheep   goat goat goat
sheep sheep sheep   goat goat goat
sheep sheep sheep   goat goat goat
sheep sheep sheep   goat goat goat
sheep sheep sheep   goat goat goat
sheep sheep sheep   goat goat goat
sheep sheep sheep   goat goat goat

WOLVES IN THE GARDEN

They had been at it all day long, so they finally stopped to catch their wind, before heading back to the tree house for supper. In those days, before sin, Adam still had wings, mighty wings, and could indeed fly with the eagles. For this wonderful, all-day-long contest, he had kept them tightly folded along his back, so the contest would be even. Adam also was physically perfect, and fully, correctly functional, just the way God had designed and built him. Always being in flawless, peak condition and strength allowed him to run at more than four times what his broken descendents would be able to achieve. Both he, and his favorite exploring partner, Wolf, could run for short times at speeds of almost 70 miles per hour, and, one time, just to see if they could really do it, they had both chased down, and touched, a running cheetah!

Well, today, they had spotted a wild mustang herd, and decided that the challenge would be who could catch seven wild horses fastest. Using a type of flower blossom that acted like modern Velcro, they would catch up to the horse, then slap the blossom on the horse's flank, as a tag, then move on. They changed the color of the Velcro flowers every new game, so they could keep accurate score. The horses actually thrilled to play the game with them, and did their wildest efforts to elude the touch of either Adam, or, especially, Wolf. Oh, everyone knew one another, and they liked Wolf well enough, but something about those scary teeth and eyes made the horses always keep a close watch on Wolf, and he always was careful around their hooves.

Adam carried the Velcro tag in his hand, but Wolf carried it in his mouth.

This made an extra challenge for the horses, since each one of them was hungry for the touch of Adam's hand, but each one was nervous about the teeth of Wolf.

They all played by the rules, though, and with no injuries, and lots of fun, excitement, and tons of good exercise for all of them. As the afternoon wore on, they all covered the large field where they played with millions of foot, paw, and hoof prints. They used up hundreds of the special flower blossoms, which could grow back a week later, here. Finally, puffing breath, as sunset neared, the man and the wolf thanked the horses for the great day of fun, and they all agreed to meet here again for a repeat contest, next week, once the marker blossoms had grown back.

Adam and Wolf turned back toward home, to the house in the tree where Adam had first met Eve, and Wolf had first met She-Wolf. This was not the same Special Tree, which the Lord had called the "Tree of Life". It was also not the forbidden tree, which the Lord had called the "Tree of the Knowledge of Good and Evil". Nonetheless, it was their special tree, and the place they lived.

As Adam and Wolf headed home, Wolf looked at Adam, and smiling a Wolf-smile, asked, "So, who won?"

Adam threw back his head, as he roared a laugh. "You did, Champ!" As soon as he heard that, Wolf began happily wagging his great tail, as he excitedly trotted along, bouncing, on his tireless, steel spring legs.

Even though the day was wonderful, and the sunset beautiful, and the weather splendid, Adam suddenly felt a cold chill hit his heart, a feeling he had never felt in all the centuries he had lived. He would later call this feeling fear. He shook it off, but hurried the pace as he and Wolf trotted the few remaining miles.

As they ran, Wolf adopted his usual lead scout position, and Adam let him increase the spacing between them to about a hundred yards. When they were about a half-mile away, they both heard a sound they never heard before. It was She-Wolf, growling, snarling, and barking, all at the top of her lungs, making the sounds that would later be known as the sounds of a life and death struggle. Both Wolf and Adam hit the afterburners, and Wolf, because of the spacing, disappeared behind the little hillside that concealed their tree from view, on this pathway.

As soon as Wolf raced behind the hill, Adam snapped out his wings to full length, almost 21 feet, and leaped into the air. He had to fly carefully, this close to all the tree limbs. He skimmed the ground, just under the branches. In a couple of seconds he zipped around the hillside, and instantly saw Eve and She-Wolf, and the rapidly receding tail of

Wolf, as he chased something out the far side of the clearing that formed the giant front yard for their home.

Adam noticed something very strange about Eve. She seemed like a different person, like she was not quite fully connected to him, or the present moment, as though lost in her own inner thoughts and schemes. Also, there was a very twisted, repulsive expression upon her face. For some reason, she resembled the snake. Strangest of all, her wings were gone, nowhere to be seen.

Adam landed smoothly in front of her, grabbed her arms, looked deep into her strange eyes, and asked, "Are you okay?"

For a few seconds, she seemed far away, but then seemed to focus on him, and answered, "Yes, I think so. That was the serpent that was here, and what Wolf is chasing."

Adam looked down at She-Wolf, and said, "Good girl! Thank you for guarding her. Stay watch here until we get back, girl."

With that, Adam once more launched into the air, and sped after Wolf, landing smoothly at the place where he had seen Wolf vanish into the forest. Adam began to run swiftly through the trees, until he emerged into a small clearing, with a large rock wall at one end of it. There was Wolf, crouched to spring, fangs bare, jaws open, with drops of saliva falling to the ground. The hackles on his neck were so upraised, that his neck fur resembled a lion's mane. A sound like a low frequency, deep earthquake was rumbling down in Wolf's throat, a sound Adam had never heard from him before.

There, with his back against the rock wall, and staring with hatred and contempt at Wolf, was the serpent. In those days, Adam could clearly see the spirits, and the twisted cherub wanted to kill Wolf, but could not, because, although Eve had just fallen, Adam still had not, and, since the good Lord gave Earth to the race of men, and since Adam was still the rightful, and righteous, King of Earth, the serpent had no power or authority over any one in the universe, except for Eve. Adam noticed that the serpent's great wings were not missing, but broken. No wonder he had not just flown away.

Adam landed, walked over to the serpent, and said, in a deep growl, very much like the one coming from Wolf, "Stay away from my wife, and my life! I don't know yet what you were up to, but I am going to find out. I will finish dealing with you, one day soon. Until then, stay away. God told me to name the creatures, and I did, and now your name is changed from "Friend", to "Enemy", and from "Lucifer", to "Satan", and from "cherub", to "devil". Get out of my Garden, and take your twisted crap with you, jerk!"

As Adam said the last word, a great funnel cloud came and grabbed the serpent, and he was yanked up, screaming curses, and disappeared into the evening sky. Adam and Wolf watched him being carried off, hearing his ugly voice fade away.

Adam turned to Wolf, and said, "I do not know what all this is about, yet, but we will understand, soon. Thank you, my friend, for being so ready to defend us in battle!"

Wolf trotted up beside Adam, and looked up at him, and said, "You know that I would die for you."

Adam replied, "Same here, Wolf! Hopefully, that will not be necessary. I do feel a deadly storm building, though."

The two trotted along in silence for a minute, and then Wolf asked, "What happened to Momma's wings?"

Adam shook his head as they ran, and then answered, "I am not sure. Somehow, we must try to get them back!"

SHADOW OF DEATH

The moonlight was so intensely bright that I could easily read the names and dates on the tombstones. It was strangely quiet, as though everything around me was sort of holding its' breath. The time was about an hour after midnight, some night in October, back in the year 1977.

I was walking back home in Denton. The evening had been spent over at a friend's house, as we watched a late football game, where a West Coast University battled against a key rival. So much time has passed, that I do not recall which schools were the ones involved in the game. My buddy's house was very close to the campus, and I had about a two mile walk to complete. The walk was quiet and uneventful, at least until I arrived at the corner of the huge graveyard by Eagle. I paused, and realized that the shortest way around the graveyard was to go straight through it. I said a brief prayer, and started diagonally across the enormous graveyard, which was the oldest and biggest one in Denton. There was absolutely no problem with visibility, and I could clearly see where the graves were planted, so I managed to avoid stepping upon any of the actual grave plots, by carefully walking around them, or, stepping wide over them. All the while, there was not even the sound of a dog barking in the night, and all I heard was the gentle whisper of the cool fall breeze.

I was about a third of the way across. The total distance was less than a mile, but it seemed much longer. Suddenly, I felt that old spooky feeling that some folks have tried to describe as the feeling that someone is watching you. This was similar unto that, but radically more intense, and urgent. I stopped a few seconds, standing between two headstones, and calmed my breathing and heartbeat. That summer I had taken a college course in yoga, and had learned some effective breathing and calming techniques. After a moment, I was ready to move on, but suddenly felt this deadly threat right behind me. I had to struggle not to turn and look over my shoulder. Again, I stopped, and calmed down, and prayed that our good Lord would protect me the rest of the way home. I knew that whatever was standing right behind me would instantly kill me if it could. I also knew it was nothing natural, or I would have heard the sound of it approaching. I somehow knew, what the thing wanted, most immediately, was for my fear to conquer me, and to make me yield to it, and actually turn around and look over my shoulder. I would not give in. I realized, deep inside, that my natural eyes would have seen nothing there in the moonlight, anyway.

    A part of the human consciousness is beyond the limits of the natural, however, and some part of me, mind, heart, spirit, or something else, could perceive that a huge thing was walking right behind me, tracking me, step for step. The thing was so tall, that its' head was lost in the stars. I did not clearly see it, but would not buckle under to fear, and so would not give it the satisfaction of turning to look, or in any other way loosing my tight grip upon my courage. There were several moments that took all of my courage and faith to keep walking, as calmly as possible, working my way across the graveyard. I could somehow perceive that the thing was dark, pitch black dark, with the kind of darkness that gobbles up and destroys the light around it.

All the time, I kept praying, partly hoping it was all just my imagination, but solidly knowing that it was very real, indeed. I do not know what would have happened, if I had not obeyed our good Lord, and just kept facing forward, marching through death in living faith.

Maybe nothing would have happened. Or, maybe, if I had looked, my courage and faith would have failed me. I suppose I might have even died of shock, if I had given in, and looked, and perhaps have clearly seen the monster that was actually there, but unseen.

I know that I felt more hatred and hostility focused upon me that night than I had ever experienced before in my lifetime. It would have crushed even my bravest efforts, if I had not also felt the tremendous love and strength that our good Lord was steadily transferring into my heart, all the way home. Either way, I could not surrender to my emotions, since I had been commanded to walk home in faith, nothing doubting.

As I finally reached the far side of the graveyard, and stopped for a minute, to let out a huge sigh of relief, I did at last turn around and look back, but not until I was standing several yards beyond the boundaries of the graveyard. You know what I saw? All I saw was a quiet, empty graveyard, well-lit in the bright moonlight, and nothing else.

That was pretty much what I expected to see. The thing that had been set to grab, rip, and tear me apart with its' ferocious claws and teeth had actually been right there, inches away from me. Just because my eyes were not able to directly see it had not in one tiny fraction diminished the savage reality. I do not know if the Lord would have let it kill me, but I know I was supposed to keep on marching, all the way across, and not let evil scare me. The only way I have ever found to have courage like that, is to immediately pray, asking the Lord for strength, and help, and then step out in faith, trusting Him to do it for me. Once I have done that, it is my responsibility to continue in the course He has set for me, whether I like the journey, or not. At least, it is good to know that He walks with us, and will certainly get us to the place He has planned for us, and do it much more quickly, when we obey, no matter what He commands for us to do. I could not have done it without His help, but we would not have done it together, without my faith and obedience. Think about that for a moment. Almighty God, Who does not need anybody, or anything, to help Him, no matter what, still finds a way to honor us who follow Him. He weaves us into His plans, and allows us to become true partners with Him, even though He always has the controlling interest. God will always be the Senior Partner, and the Chairman of the Board. How amazing is it that He would even take the thought, or the time, to arrange events and works where we are allowed to join with His plan, and to do so voluntarily?

What I learned, among other things, is that I am to obey, even if I do not understand, and that I am to trust His instructions, and work steadily toward the successful conclusion that is the objective. God shows us the wonderful way He achieves not only His goals, but also our own. My goal was to safely walk home from my friend's house. I did not plan to march through the graveyard, though; that just sort of happened.

God's plan also included getting me home safely, even though He made the journey very scary, and, indeed, almost allowed me to be killed by terror and shock. I think the main part of His goal was to get me to trust and obey Him. God was able to accomplish both goals very satisfactorily.

I did not understand why the perception of the enemy was marked mostly by its' evil, and deadly threat, and destructive intent, but also by its' stunning size and height. The answer was given to me many years later, as I read Ezekiel one day, and noticed how the cherubs of God, of which the enemy used to be one, were characterized as being so tall that when they stand upon the Earth, their heads are in the stars. When I read that, even though many years had passed, I felt a cold chill, deep in my heart, and I knew that what I had experienced that night had been entirely real. Something evil, and as tall as the sky, had wanted to kill me that night.

The only thing that prevented my death that night in the graveyard was that Someone bigger than the sky was also standing there, also unseen by my eyes, but the enemy saw Him, all right. There is a scene in the Disney movie, The Bear, in which a mountain lion is about to kill a little baby bear cub. The lion closes in for the kill, and even swats the baby bear's nose, ripping a wound into the little bear's face. Of course, the baby is screaming in fear and desperation, hoping for rescue. Suddenly the lion loses all courage, and flees the scene, running for its' life. The camera backs up, and there standing a few yards behind the baby bear, is a huge adult grizzly bear, roaring death against the lion. The lion believed the big bear meant it, and left the baby bear alone.

As I noted before, many lessons were taught that night. I learned that I am to trust and obey the Lord, even if I do not understand His reasons. I also learned that He is very trustworthy, even in the deadliest situations. Of course, He could have just lifted me across the graveyard, but He wanted me to walk through it with Him.

I was not the only one who learned a lesson from Him that night. The enemy learned that whenever he thinks it is a good time to try to kill me, Someone bigger than the sky is standing right there with me. The one thing that can make this baby show courage greater than a lion is to know that my defender never leaves me alone in battle. One day, the enemy will forever leave me alone. For all eternity, the good Lord never will leave me alone, and I am very, very glad!

OUT OF THE MAIN SEQUENCE

Astronomers use a method to plot the various stars according to their mass and luminosity. The stars are plotted with a horizontal axis for mass, versus a vertical axis for luminosity. Starting at the lower left corner, the smallest, dimmest stars are gathered. At the diagonal opposite corner, the upper right, are clustered the large, bright stars. All along the connecting plot between the two extremes, stars increase in size and brightness, as they are placed further upwards, to the upper right corner. So, in a nutshell, red dwarves are at the lowest left corner, and blue-white super giants, at the extreme upper right. All along the stretch from one extreme to the other, various-sized, and various-brightness stars grow bigger and brighter as they go up the path.

The colors of the stars indicate their temperatures, and range from the coolest, dim red, to bright red, orange, yellow (actually, green, since "yellow" is, by scientific definition, a reflective color, and the projective color, green, is the component of our Sun's light that our eyes perceive as "yellow", until it reflects off of a green surface) and white, all the way to blue-white (a blue so intense that it registers as mostly white).

The color of dead stars is black, if they have collapsed into singularities. If not, then they give back no more light than any planet would, which is only reflective.

There are some unusual stars, however, which do not fit into the primary groupings of most other stars. These are exampled by white dwarves, and red super giants. White dwarves, because they are bright, are near the top of the chart, but, since they have low mass, compared to other stars, they are to the left of the chart, on the same side as red dwarves. Red super giants are on the right side of the chart, the same side as the blue-white super giants, but they are near the bottom of the graph, because they are not bright stars. (Actually, the total luminosity of a star is a mathematical function of its' total surface area, as well as its' brightness, so in the case of red super giants, they still put out a lot of light, even though it is red.)

The primary pathway, where most of the "normal" stars are located, is called the Main Sequence. ("Normal" is the scientific term for "average".)

Strange stars, such as white dwarves and red super giants, are therefore said to fall outside the main sequence.

Stars are so uniquely individual, that each separate one can be distinguished by its' own particular color spectrum, depending upon the precise balance of various elements within that particular star. The stars are similar in some ways unto snowflakes. Each one is wonderfully unique, and yet they are all very, very similar, and mankind has a challenging task to distinguish one from another, though with modern equipment, it can be done.

There are similarities between stars and human beings, too. Of course, we know these days that our physical atoms and elements came from past supernovae, and are the leftover dust from ancient stars which grew unstable, and exploded.

There is more to it than just that, though. When a star ignites, and fires up, for the first time, a new light blazes forth into the darkness, and the darkness runs from it. When a Christian is born again, by the grace of God, and is allowed to believe in Jesus, which is a privilege, and an undeserved free gift, from God, and the new believer, in humble response, chooses to live for, follow, and obey Jesus, no matter what, then a new light blazes forth into the spiritual darkness of this present world. Within the spiritual realm, some things have a mind of their own, however, and this time, the sneaky things in the darkness try to cluster around the new believer, and snuff out the new light in his heart. (If we are determined, and sincere, then the Holy Spirit will preserve our faith, and Jesus will defend us, and, in His Own time, in His Own Way, our Father will rescue and restore us.)

Just as with stars, each Christian is unique, and we each have a special, One-on-one relationship with Jesus. Every Christian must find his own path to peace and harmony with our Lord. The Word gives us specific directions, and the Holy Spirit gives us extra leadings, with dreams and visions, and pictures in our minds and hearts.

Some Christians are very much part of the main sequence of Christianity. There is nothing wrong with that, as long as the One that they take their own personal marching orders from is Jesus, and not a human preacher. Humans, no matter how sincere, and no matter how Christian, can still make mistakes, and sometimes very costly ones. In this fallen world, we are all still-not-perfected, yet. We're not quite as horrible as we used to be, at least. (Well, hopefully not, anyway!)

There are some Christians that find it impossible, or at least, very uncomfortable, to try to fit into the mold of modern Christianity. Some people have substituted "Church-ianity" for actual Christianity. Some people think that one's faith is measured by one's church attendance. Some people think that one's faith is measured by one's hairstyle, or, in the case of men, one's hair length, or, in the case of women, one's skirt length. Some people think you are not really a Christian, unless you are dunked fully under water, although there is absolutely no literal Scriptural authority to support that claim. King

Jesus told us clearly that even circumcision, or the lack thereof, did not matter to Him, but what was in a person's heart, and what they secretly delighted in, and what they set their heart upon, were the things which He counted. Do not take my word for it; read His Word, for your self.

So, there are some folks that do indeed love our Lord, but do not perhaps do it in the way to which we are accustomed. We are not supposed to judge them, and if you read James, you will see that for your self.

Also, work more on that beam in your own eye, instead of worrying about that tiny speck in someone else's eye.

The unusual Christians therefore can be considered outside the main sequence, but they are still stars, and each one of them shines with his, or her, own special, unique light, just like you do. We still each have some individual gifts given to us by Him, and we are each to seek and find the best ways to use those gifts to bring King Jesus honor.

Listen, I spent about fourteen years of my life with a ponytail down to my belt. I also, at times, have had a beard down to my chest which would make ZZ Top proud. I always rode big motorcycles, until my spine said that it had spent enough years doing that, and would I please let it stop? I played drums in several different groups, in Texas and California. Now given all of that, do you possibly think that I would ever fit snugly into the main sequence of modern Christianity?

Of course not! I have been going to my present church for almost three years, and my hair and my beard are both very short, and always neatly trimmed, but that's because I lived through enough miserable summers in Texas with long hair and a thick beard. Nonetheless, I look about "normal" again, now, and even though I am okay about regular attendance, and giving, you can bet I still get a whole lot of very strange looks from a whole lot of the other people at church, every time I go there, though most are friendly, and sort of curious, like when they take their kids to see strange creatures at the zoo!

No, I will never again in my life be a strictly main sequence Christian, even though my parents raised me very "normally" in the church. I have traveled too far, and seen and heard far too much, and I can never be crammed down into the cookie cutter again.

Even with all of that, our good Lord has still found a few uses for me in His service. I have been given, and still am being given, some wonderful opportunities to do a good thing, here or there, maybe nothing big, but something that shows God's goodness unto someone else, and does not expect a return trade-off gift back to me. If I can give, or do, something to bless someone else, and do it cleanly, with no selfish motive or pride in it for me, then our good Lord can have the glory, and that allows me a way to help bring a blessing unto Him. That's very, very cool with me. I mean, after all, He hung naked on a cross, taking my place, with spikes driven through His wrists and feet, until the Romans killed Him, when all the time it should have been me hanging there on that cross. Just by paying for my worthless life, with His Own priceless life, He has already given me more honor than I can ever repay to Him.

So, just because someone is not precisely the "type" or "sort" of Christian you expect them to be, do not think poorly of them. God has always found a way to utilize the very people that would perfectly accomplish the mission which He assigned them, no matter what their background, nationality, race, or personal history. The primary requirement is that they love our good Lord enough to take

Him seriously, and actually do what He tells us to do, and not to just talk about it, but not do it. Notice how many times our good Lord told off the hypocrites. He does not like hypocrites.

When you notice that you are mentally placing the stars around you in their proper filing arrangement on the chart, and you automatically try to fit everyone into someplace on the main sequence, remember to leave room at the corners for those special strange stars which are outside the main sequence. God made them, too, and gave each of us our own special light, to shine for Him.

Also, remember that the apostles did not start out as very holy men themselves. All throughout the history of the world, and Israel, in particular, God has often used men and women that most folks thought of little value. God is able to see things in people that even the people themselves can not see, and neither can anyone else, except God. God is also able to work great miracles through even little people, those whom the world counts as nobodies.

Something else I will share with you is this: when we look up into the night sky, the magnificent beauty and scope of it all takes away our breath, and stuns us into wonder. When our good Lord looks down from His Throne upon a dark and evil world, He can see brightly glowing stars all over the dark world: individuals, and galaxies, and super-clusters of galaxies of dazzling, fiercely blazing believers, all over the world, day and night, loving Him, thanking Him, blessing Him, and showing others in the darkness that God is real, and that the real God is very, very good indeed! When astronauts look down on the night side of Earth, they can see the city lights. When God looks down here, He can see even more, much brighter lights shining His truth into a dark, lying world!

Shine on, brothers and sisters. Tell the truth, and be good unto others. Follow Him, all the Way home!

TRUE, NOBLE, JUST, PURE, LOVELY, OF GOOD REPORT, PRAISEWORHTY:

These are the things we are supposed to think upon. I am thinking about them, and I noticed that there are seven total items listed. This is perhaps a parallel concept to the seven gifts of the Holy Spirit. Is there a correlation in the two lists? Let's examine them, and see.

Now, we know that every Word of God is pure, and so we can trust that He put them in the order that He wanted them. The first of the gifts is listed as prophecy, and that certainly does correspond directly to true. Again and again, ever since Genesis, God has been proving His prophecies to be true. He will continue to do so.

The next listed gift is healing. When King Jesus was here, as The Evangelist, He was also already here as the next rightful King of Israel. One of the aspects of being a king is that a king must protect and help his people. King Jesus came to protect His people from the consequences of their own sins, and to set them free from oppression, and to heal their sicknesses and wounds, and also, to drive demons out of them. These things were done with the primary intent of solid witness proof of His Holy Identity, as God. Even so, the things which He did, and the manner in which He did them, all shout "King of kings! Lord of lords! This Fellow is Almighty God, as a Man!" King Jesus showed the greatest nobility of all, when He healed us all of a death sentence, by giving, willingly, His Own priceless life for all of us. So, yes, healing and nobility do indeed correspond.

What about teaching? How is that just? Well, remember how Jesus said that we would all be taught by God? A believer is someone who has been taught, by God, that Jesus is the Christ. Remember how Jesus also said, since we freely received, we must freely give. In most contexts, this is viewed as referring to mercy, but is there any more effective way to teach someone that King Jesus is God, than by showing them mercy, since He freely gave it to us? Also, it is only just for us to obey our Lord, since He gave His life for us. So, yes, teaching others about Christ does indeed correspond to justice.

What about exhortation? How does that ever match up with pure? Think about exhortation to worship God (not manipulation to send money to a televangelist, to keep him on the air). When we exhort people to draw closer to God, and to talk to Him, and to listen to Him, and to obey Him, and to walk with Him, and to stick with Him, then we are not seeking a selfish gain at all. We genuinely want them to be blessed by knowing our good Lord better, and we want to have the same blessing for ourselves. One of the best ways we can know Him better, is to exhort others to worship and love Him, also. So, yes, exhortation does indeed correspond to purity.

How about giving? Is there any observable tie with lovely? I must say, I think our good Lord is both instructing us, and also sharing a pun with us, which would only be possible in these last days, and in English! (I told you that He has a great sense of humor.) While the act of someone generously giving some much needed help to a person in dire straights is a beautiful, and "lovely" sight to witness, and it is usually done by a "lovely" person, whether man, or woman, or child, there is one more perspective. It is also an act of genuine love, even more toward the King, than toward the person being helped. Still, for the person being granted the help, it is definitely a work of love, and renews hope. So, it is "lovely" in that sense, also. So, yes giving and lovely do definitely match up.

What does leadership, or authority, have to do with something being of good report? Well, if the leader, or person in authority, is of good report, it is because he has ruled well and wisely, and with respect for those under his authority. Any leader is heavily in the spotlight, all the time, 24 hours a day, 7 days a week, and even on vacation, if they ever get one of those. The people that are not in charge think it would be great to be boss, and it would be, except for all the tons of extra work and hassle that goes with it. Don't believe me? Ask any leader, if he has time to answer you! At any rate, no one is more frequently praised, or criticized, than a leader. Everyone else thinks that he could do it better. So, the reports will always be generated, some good, some bad. If the leader is good, he will be of good report. If not, then God will remove him after a while. So, does leadership, or authority, have much to do with things of good report? It most certainly better, if it wants to stay in authority!

Last, but absolutely not least, we must consider mercy. It is easily observable that showing mercy is indeed praiseworthy, especially because it is often very difficult, even nearly impossible, if the person has hurt you badly enough. When a person can release his anger, and, (only by remembering the grace of God, in forgiving his own sin) choose to extend mercy to those that have harmed him, we all must cheer, and give him a standing ovation, even though he is, like each of us, only an unprofitable servant, merely doing that which it is his responsibility to perform. Still, I think the case is clearly made that mercy is, without doubt, praiseworthy, and does follow the example and commandment of

Jesus, namely, that we love one another, as He loved us, with mercy!

Once again, the marvelous Creator has revealed yet another interwoven mystery of deep truth about Himself, and His wondrous Ways, hidden deep within His many-layered Word. It is the glory of God to conceal a thing, but the honor of kings is to search things out. Our Biggest Brother, King Jesus, promised that He would make us kings, also, one Day. For now, it is good practice for us to keep on searching out hidden mysteries in His Word. Beside that, we might actually learn something worth knowing!

AUTOMATIC IDOLATRY

The most effective weapon technology involves more than a single characteristic. Effective systems must include target acquisition, tracking, propulsion, and payload, to name the basics. Also, a weapon is of no use, if it is not effective, no matter how accurate it may be. So, an effective weapon must accurately deliver a lethal payload precisely to the designated target, and must accomplish the total destruction of the target, or render it inactive.

In modern warfare, although the same is true in ancient warfare, a weapon that can get close to its' target without being detected is of prime value. An invisible plane cannot be shot down, and a silent, deep submarine cannot be attacked. Military commanders have been using various forms of camouflage, quite successfully, for thousands of years, even back to pre-historic times, wearing animal skins to sneak close to game animals when hunting.

In spiritual battle, similar principles apply. The one that launches unseen (but still deadly and real) missiles of hurt at us is the enemy. A sort of nasty "shot in the dark" can be fired at a person's heart, mind, body, or at any other blessing in the person's life, to try to destroy the target, or at least render it inactive. Even worse, oftentimes the attack is directed against the target's loved ones, also. Evil is cruel, and heartless, and that is why Jesus will utterly destroy it, soon.

The first, and still, the most effective, weapon which the enemy fired at humans was temptation, in the form of a lie. It was camouflaged as truth, and falsely called wisdom, by the lying enemy, as it murdered Eve's soul, and enslaved her mind to serve it, by disguising itself as her own best interests. Eve was taught to want whatever she wanted, and to spare no effort or trick to acquire it for her self. She did not realize that her real new god was the devil, since it had cleverly disguised itself as Eve, herself, at least, in her own mind, and in her now-twisted heart. Right after that, it was able to persuade her to murder the soul of her husband, also. After all, she did not want to go to hell alone. Shouldn't her husband be willing to go there with her, if he really loved her?

Poor Eve, indeed, and since all of the rest of us, except Jesus Christ, have also sinned, and fallen short of the glory of God, for that matter, pity all the rest of us, too. At least, it would have gone that way, if not for Jesus killing the dragon.

The weapon of temptation is always camouflaged, and is usually right up next to its' target, before it is noticed, and sometimes, the surprise attack can succeed, if the target is caught off-guard. That is why Paul instructed Timothy to flee temptation, not to try to resist it. It is only possible for Jesus, and the Holy Spirit, to actually conquer temptation. Jesus did it by applying the Holy Scripture, and refusing to bow down to the enemy, since the enemy is, after all, only a made thing, not the One Who is the Maker. Only the Maker Himself is worthy of worship, but not anything that He created! (That includes any human at all, except Jesus, Who is actually God. You are not Jesus, and neither am I, so that list of those unworthy of worship also includes you, and me, too!)

We are instructed to resist the devil, and it will flee from us. We are also told to draw near to God, and He will draw near to us. We are clearly told not to mess with temptation, however, but to leave it behind, before being drawn into it. Remember that Jesus warned Peter, James, and John to pray, lest they enter into temptation. In this world, temptations will come, but we are to flee from them immediately, if possible, and pray for strength to not enter into temptation, at any rate.

In spiritual effect, temptation can be considered a kind of a black hole, such that when one is drawn in, there is little possibility of escape, and the end result is death and darkness. We humans always think we can "handle" it. Remember the old potato chip commercial that said, "Bet you can't eat just one?" Every successful drug dealer also knows that he has to give the first few samples away for free, to get the new user involved, as a way of life. Then the price can go as high as the dealer wants to set it.

As far as weapons go, it has all the characteristics of effectiveness. No external device is needed, once the person's mindset is already biased toward rebellion and selfishness. The person's wicked heart will fixate upon, and work to implement, the end result, erroneously imagined as something wonderful, but it will not bear good fruit, ultimately, since the seed was made evil by being planted for a selfish, evil purpose. The person's own mind hears the set of temptations that are most likely to succeed, in that person's mind, since the person giving in, to do something, wants to succeed at it, and not get caught. So, lust, or selfishness, sparks the fire, and temptation fans the flames, and sin roars into action, bringing forth death, and the target is neutralized, or enslaved, for evil uses.

Even though it is an ugly word, it nonetheless needs to be said. It is "idolatry." That is precisely what it boils down to, when a person worships them selves, and what they want, more than God, and what He wants. Why do you think Jesus kept telling us to put others first, and even gave us His life to show us how, and to prove that He meant it? The original sin was covetousness, which is a fancy word for selfishness. The enemy selfishly wanted to steal God's glory, and to force creation to worship it, instead of God. The enemy wanted everybody to believe its' lies, instead of God's truth.

So, when a person listens unto their own desires, and deliberately goes against God's commands, that person is, without realizing it, actually worshipping an idol, instead of God. All idol worship is really devil worship, in camouflage. To worship one's own self, is to worship something besides Jesus. That is, by definition of terms, idolatry, and devil worship. The devil has been launching that missile, ever since the events in the Garden of Eden, and it is only by the grace of our good Lord that any of us have been allowed to escape death in the Lake of Fire. Anyone who commits sin is the slave of sin, and if says he has never sinned, unless that person is actually Jesus Christ, then the sinner is a liar, too.

The weapon of temptation therefore causes a type of automatic idolatry. That is very, very nasty, indeed. Since it is difficult to spot, and hard to resist, the best defense against temptation is to pray, and flee, little human! Trust in Jesus, and run to Him, and away from death!

FIRSTBORN

A fine afternoon in late summer was a great opportunity for the wolf puppy and the bear cub to chase and wrestle, each one testing his speed and strength against his friend. They were within a day of the same age, and had grown up as neighbors and playmates, exploring the whole mountainside, as far as their mothers would let them go. The mothers were also friends, as were the daddies. The mothers gossiped all day, as they watched and fed the babies, while the big boys were out exploring on their own, acting just like their little sons tried to act, back home on the gentle part of the slope, on the side of a lush, green mountain. There were all sorts of animals there, and all lived well in harmony, ever since about a hundred years ago, when the Son of God, Jesus Christ, had returned with all of the resurrected and transfigured saints who had loved Him, and also the good cherubs, and all the good angels, too. The world, and all Creation, was finally at peace, and no one started any fights, and even disagreements were usually civil enough, and only rarely did a spark of the old enemy, pride, ever try to rise again, but it was always instantly squashed by the Sons of Light, who went around reminding the whole Earth that "Jesus is God!" Reminded of that, every creature immediately relaxed back to humility, and obedience, at the sound of the Name above all names.

With no danger to anyone, or anything, since sin and evil were locked up in the bottomless pit (actually a singularity, large enough to keep over 1,000 galaxies held captive within its' dark gravity well), the cubs and pups could play without concern, except to not fall over the side of the cliff. Living creatures could still feel lots of pain, even if most of the time, they recovered fairly quickly.

Although they were the same age, about six months, the bear was already growing larger and stronger, even though he had started out smaller. As they wrestled and play-fought, suddenly the bear cub used his increased strength without realizing it, and swatted his wolf friend's nose, way too hard, and actually slashed a cut into the baby wolf's nose. The puppy howled in pain, and shock! No one had ever hurt him that much before, and certainly not his best buddy, Bear.

The two mothers were a ways off, but clearly heard the wolf's little cry. They both sprinted the hundred yards or so to the babies, but the wolf mother far outraced the bear, since she was much faster, and it was her own baby's cry. As she came over the small rise, and screeched to a halt, she saw the bear standing in front of her baby, and even though the little bear was as stunned by his friend's injury as the wolf baby was, it did not look at all like that, in a glance, to the mother wolf. She leaped over to the little bear, and, using her own head like a battering ram, knocked him away from her baby. She had not been trying to hurt him, but had just used enough force to move him about ten feet away, which was accomplished by sending him rolling backwards, like a little fur ball, until he stopped up against a tree limb.

Meanwhile, the mother bear arrived on the scene, and disliked what she saw, even more intensely. Just as the little bear cub was rolling to a stop against the fallen tree, his mother charged into her friend, the wolf mother, and sent her flying about twenty feet through the air, and not at all gently. The wolf landed nimbly on her mighty feet, and snarled. She began, with hackles raised, to advance to battle with her friend. The babies, by this time, had forgotten their own incident, which had triggered all of this chain reaction, and they were huddled together in fear, whimpering for their mothers to stop fighting, and let's go home, okay?

Even though the maternal radar inside the hearts and minds of the two mothers was still locked on target with each of their own babies, they faced each other, as they circled and snarled. Neither one really wanted to be the first one to try to kill her friend, but a mom's got to do what a mom's got to do, right?

Suddenly, the huge male wolf broke into the clearing, and like a grey missile, launched himself at the bear, since he thought she was threatening both his mate, and his baby. He hit her like a living ton of bricks, and even though he only weighed about 250 pounds, it was all solid muscle, and teeth, and he managed to knock the bear over backwards, and, in a flash, was at her throat, and ready to kill. His jaws had the crushing power of over a ton per square inch, and he was locked onto her throat, all the way up to his molars. The bear weighed about twice what he weighed, but he had the throat-hold advantage, and she instantly quit struggling, knowing, at a gut level, that he could easily rip out her throat, as though there were no thick neck fur there at all, since his long fangs had easily gone right through all of that, and much deeper. The bear could feel the overwhelming strength in his jaws, impossible to fight free from, and the razor teeth were not dug in to her hide yet, because he was holding back, but in a split second, they both knew he could kill her. She forced herself to relax, knowing somehow that he would not do her any harm, but was just sort of making an arrest, until he found out what all the fuss was. It might have ended there, a few seconds later, when they all had a chance to sort things out, but the crashing arrival of the big male bear, also a slower runner than the wolves, triggered a whole new set of catastrophes. The bear also skidded to a halt, but it took him longer, since he weighed over half a ton. As he was stopping, raising a cloud of dust, he saw and grasped instantly that his mate was in a death hold, and was maybe about to die. The bear also knew enough to realize that he could not possibly make the wolf let her survive, or forcibly remove the wolf's teeth from her throat, since that would also rip out her throat. Bears are ruthless, and smart, and, in a flash, the bear knew he needed leverage. He turned toward the wolf puppy, and began to move menacingly toward the puppy and the she-wolf. The mother wolf instantly understood, and snatched her terrified baby up in her own jaws, and hauled him out of there, knowing it was the only way to save his life. Her mate could handle the mother bear alone. All right, but she did not want to battle the big male bear at all. As she raced away with a desperation and speed born of adrenaline, and terror of death, not for herself, but for her baby, the huge grizzly came roaring after them, and, even though it took him a while to get moving, he could attain speeds of up to 40 miles an hour, for short runs. That much muscle can get even a massive beast moving pretty well.

She planned as she ran, and headed uphill, which was extra exhausting, and she knew that a wolf can run for hours, and even days at a time, but a bear cannot. Still, she was carrying Junior, and he was getting to be a large baby these days. Still, it looked like she was going to make it over the mountain top, when suddenly, she stepped into an unseen hole in the rocks, and tripped, and both she and her puppy went sprawling across the ground, and had to each grab for footing, to avoid rolling back down the mountain. As she looked back, the grizzly was still huffing and puffing up the mountainside, and he was determined, having seen her trip and fall. The wolf grabbed her pup again, and off she went, but a little slower on her sore foot. The bear was gaining on them, now. She could hear his loud breath closer behind them, and stopped, and put the puppy down, and screamed "RUN!!!" at him, then turned to stop the bear. The little wolf started to run away, but then stopped and looked back. Why wasn't his mother coming with him?

Then the bear crashed out of the trees, moving like a freight train, and roaring like a tornado. Just as he was about six feet away from a very brave and determined-to-kill mother wolf, the bear suddenly felt himself grabbed by the fur at the back of his neck, just like a little baby kitten, and he instantly went limp, when he heard a man's voice roar like a lightning crash at the back of his head, "STOP! Jesus Christ will NOT tolerate this in our world, evermore!"

The bear was curious just what had happened, and who had lifted him and shaken him like a little rag doll, but he was not able to move, to try to turn and see the person or thing behind him. Strangely, the bear felt no fear, and no more anger, either, but somehow he felt ashamed, as though he had let down his dearest friend.

The bear looked down between his own feet, and saw the treetops below, as the person lifted him higher. He saw the wolf and her puppy, both all right, and barking excitedly, wagging their tails, and bouncing all over the place, trying to follow the man up into the air. Instead, they tracked his flight down the mountainside, as he swiftly carried the bear back to where it all started.

The bear saw them landing, but when his paws touched, he did not move much at all, except to sit down and be very still, and quiet. Ever since the man had shouted the Name of the Lord at him, the bear had been very calm and well-behaved. The man came around from behind him, and looked him in the eye, and said, "I will have no more of that, for the rest of your life. You were created with great strength, to help others, not to hurt them. Now behave, and do not make me kill you, okay?" The bear nodded humbly, and hung his enormous head in shame, and began to weep quietly, as he looked over at his mate, and his cub, and thought it would be sad if he got in trouble again, and his little family would not have a daddy any more, if the man killed him.

Suddenly, the whole wolf family came together into the clearing, and sat down, a few feet away. The cub and the pup immediately came up to each other, sniffing noses, and checking to see if they were each okay. The little wolf's nose was almost healed already, and was just a little tender pink scratch by now. The mothers also took their cue from the babies, and came up to each other, sobbing softly, each one delighted to see that her best friend had not been killed by her own mate.

The big boys were last, and the wolf did not come all the way up to the bear, or touch noses with him, but just came up and sat down right in front of him, and, without a word, tilted his head sideways as he looked at his best friend, deep in the eyes, and, at last, said, "Are you okay, Bear? And what were you thinking, anyway?"

At these questions, the bear let out a huge sob, and began to bawl like a great big baby, blubbering about how he was a no-good bear, and was not a friend to anybody, most of all Wolf, and he was very, very sorry, and would Wolf and his family ever forgive his insanity?

Wolf threw back his mighty head, and literally howled with laughter. "Forgive? I am just very glad that we are all okay, and that Abel just happened to be flying around these mountains today!"

The bear dried some of his tears with his paws, and said, as he looked around at the gigantic man, standing about 14 feet tall, with great wings of light and gold, and a face that shined like the sun, "Abel?"

Wolf laughed again, and said, "Yes, the famous Prince Abel, the Firstborn Man of Faith, in God, and he was the son of King Adam, and Queen Eve! His name means 'My Daddy is God!'"

Abel nodded and smiled, and said, "Nice to meet you, Bear. So, do you guys have all of this about sorted out?"

Bear nodded enthusiastically, and answered, "Yes, sir. We will never have a problem again, at least not out of me!"

Abel gave a wry laugh, as he stretched his wings, and leaped up into the air, hovering there for a second.

"Even though all evil is locked up in the pit right now, pride still tries to make an escape every once in a while. It is the slipperiest of sins, and contention comes only by pride. The King will no longer tolerate such a lie in our world, any more, forever!"

Abel flew a little bit higher, and said, "I will come back and check on you in a while. I want to see how those boys are growing up! Good to see you again, Wolf!"

Abel flew swiftly away, headed back toward New Jerusalem, since he had a party to attend there, later that evening. A squad of 24 angels flew alongside him. They left glowing streaks of light, as they flew higher and higher, headed eastward.

Bear turned to Wolf, and said, "So, you know Prince Abel, the Firstborn?"

Wolf laughed, and replied, "Yes, we were friends, a long time ago. She-wolf and I were the pets of the Royal Family. We used to live with them in the first Garden, before the fall!"

Bear shook his head, and said, "But you always looked like just any ordinary wolf."

Wolf smiled, then began to grow much larger, until he towered over Bear, and glowed brighter and brighter, as his muscles and fangs grew even greater and larger still. Bear looked up at his friend, revealed in his glory, and trembled, and whispered, "I never knew."

Wolf replied, "I try to keep it hidden. It is easier to live a sort of normal life this way, and teach Junior how to be a wolf, before he learns to be a super-wolf. These wings, for instance, have their uses, but are not for everyday work."

They glanced over at the baby wolf, and laughed at his stunned-with-wonder expression, as he saw his father, for the first time in his life, with his glory revealed.

Seeing his son's thought clearly, Wolf answered the unasked question, and said, "Yes, little wolf. When you are all grown up, since you are the son of royal wolves, you will have wings, too!"

Bear suddenly smacked himself in the forehead with his paw just like a human does, and said, "Wait a minute! You said that you and She-wolf were both the pets of the royal family. Does that mean that she, too, is, uh…?"

"Special?"

Bear turned around, and standing there behind him, silent as a whisper, was another gigantic, deadly, monster wolf, just like Wolf. She-wolf smiled down at Bear, as the thought entered his bear-mind that She-wolf could have easily killed him, if she had thought it was necessary.

She-wolf smiled down at Bear, and said, "Yes, friend Bear. Abel did not stop you to save me. He grabbed you before I had to kill you."

SEASONED WITH SALT

The earliest of my ocean memories happened in 1955 and 1956, in Galveston, Texas. We lived in Houston, at the time, and we often drove down on Friday evening during the summers. All the men of our neighborhood were usually home from work by 1700 or 1800, so most of the families went there as a caravan, bringing kids, dogs, fishing poles, tackle boxes, inflatable things, jellyfish sting salve, old fashioned can openers, and old fashioned steel cans to open with them. We also had things to barbecue on the beach that night, since we usually got there in an hour, and had almost another two hours of daylight for all the kids (us) to splash around in the surf for a while, before supper. I remember our parents building big campfires on the sand, and us roasting hot dogs and marshmallows in those fires, while the serious barbecue they did on coal, in little portable cookers. Sometimes, after a fresh fish had been scaled and cleaned, it was wrapped in foil, and buried in the hot coals of the campfire, after it had burned down a bit. Potatoes were also cooked like that, as were mixed veggies. Crabs, I remember, and all other shellfish, were taken back to our neighborhood in Houston, and then kept overnight, ice-chilled, and then were all boiled the next day, after the poison spot had been cut out of the crabs.

Sometimes, if the weather was not too turbulent, or the surf too wild, and if no rain was expected, a lot of our families would stay, and camp very comfortably, and informally, right there on the sand, next to our cars. Sometimes there were as many as a dozen families that stayed and camped overnight. One Saturday morning, my Dad, and some of the other men, met a man who owned a shrimp boat, a fellow named Alfred. Alfred was a very nice fellow, and had about four kids of his own, and he invited all of us to go out to fish with him and his family. He never charged us anything for it, but said he was going to go out anyway with his own folks, and the boat was plenty big enough, so, the more, the merrier!

That was where I caught my first fish, too. Dad and Mom had bought me a little plastic child's fishing rod and reel, about a third the size of a real one. After all, I was only five.

They baited my hook for me, and let me troll off of the stern, along side all of the grown ups. For a long time nothing happened, and then, suddenly, something tried to pull the rod out of my little grip. Not so fast, buster! I yelled something, already determined to drag the whale onboard, before it dragged me overboard. I was wrestling with the sea monster, and not giving up, and all the adults were telling so many instructions to me at once, that I had to shut them off, from my thoughts, so I could focus. A few minutes later, I had reeled the thing in close enough, so that we could see it, and a little closer, and one of the guys that worked on Alfred's crew (a few of them also came on Saturdays, to help run the ship) reached over the side, and grabbed the fish with a big net on a long pole, and pulled it on board. At last, we could see that it was only a little fish, not even two feet long, but it was a baby hammerhead shark!

I vaguely recall comments like, "The baby caught a baby!" and the like, and I guess it was true, but I did not get to feel much like a mighty fisher man, when that dumb neighbor of ours said that a few times. Finally, I think I remember saying, defiantly, as I stuck my tongue out at him, most maturely, "Oh yeah? Well, you're mean!"

That made my Dad laugh with pride, and he said to the neighbor, "Guess he told you, huh?" After that, the man kept his mouth shut, and I was able to savor my great first fish story victory. Of course, the baby shark also had a great story to tell all of his friends, since we had carefully removed the hook, and sent him home to his mother, too.

All of the fun things we did then are forever engraved in my mind, as some of the coolest experiences of my life. The fish and crabs and shrimp were all eaten, and made life wonderful, in their way, but the intense impact that the open waters of the Gulf of Mexico, and the raw beauty of it, both on the water, and on the beach, and the smell of salt in the air, became burned deep into the fabric of my memories. There is always something more intense, vaster, deeper, wider, and more majestic about things on and next to the ocean, things which land environments cannot equal. The sun is brighter, and hotter, the sky is bluer, and the wind is cleaner, and cooler, and smells (always) of salt. The stars are brighter, the sunrises more magnificent, the sunsets more eternal, and spectacular, with a green flash of the momentary afterimage as the sun snaps the last rays below the horizon, on a clear evening.

The ongoing spectacle, of dual endless blue horizons, one being the sky, and the other being the sea, was further continued, in major, serious, full-time, as-a-way-of-life mode, as soon as I entered the Navy, in 1971. It had been 15 long years, but my old friend the ocean had waited for me patiently, knowing he would see me, yet again. This time our journeys together would last much longer, at times until my eyes were so sick and tired of seeing only endless blue, that I actually craved the sight of green trees and fields once again. Something about the human physiology needs to see sunlight reflecting off of rich, thick green growth, since, for one needed benefit, this particular combination of reflected colors, at high intensity, triggers the natural formation of serotonin. That's not all. After a long time, sailors just get homesick, for land. After all, none of us was born out in the middle of the ocean. Even if someone had been, would they have spent their entire childhood and adolescence on the water? (Okay, maybe there are a few rare cases, but not many.)

On the subject of color environments, and their psych effects, our ships were painted Navy fleet gray, all over, everywhere, inside, and out. All you ever saw was either a lot of blue, or a lot of gray. No wonder we were hungry to see forests again! Of course, every once in a while, we passed by some island, or other, and came close enough to take navigation sightings of the lighthouse, and so, occasionally, we saw a patch of green, for a little while, but we always kept on sailing by it, watching it fade away behind.

The best colors we found were the sunsets, and sunrises, and so, these were very popular events with us, and everyone tried to take at least a few steps outside, around then, if not locked on a duty station, at the moment.

There were more wonders to behold than I can recall, but I will try to recount some of them. I once sailed within a half a mile of a waterspout, or a sea tornado, which was silently lifting a thick, dark, twisting column of water straight up into the air, where it vanished into sick-looking, dark green clouds. The column rose about 500 feet or so before disappearing. I wondered where all that water was going, since it was not raining a drop, any where around us. The best "guess-timate" of the diameter of the water column was at least two hundred yards wide, given the distance our ship was when we passed it. I momentarily wondered if our Captain had gone insane, and was trying to kill us all, but, as I watched, I noticed that we were on the back side of the track of the funnel, and it was moving away from us. Still, that was a gutsy move, even if we were on a tight schedule. I was glad that I had not run screaming onto the bridge, yelling, "Tornado, tornado!" like I would have done, back home in Texas.

There was the time when we went to a port called Bandar Abbas, in Iran. At the time, in 1974, the Shah was still in power, and the U.S. was friends with him, and it was a show of support, since Arabia had been doing some saber-rattling at Iran, and it had made the Shah nervous. Our ship was so big, with a 25 foot draft, that it could not even enter their little shallow water seaport. That was the biggest, and best, naval port in Iran, at the time. It still is the main naval port, but I am quite sure major upgrades have been done, in the last 36 years. Anyway, we had to anchor out in the middle of the Persian Gulf, and take motor whaleboats in to the beach. There was a lot of phosphorescence in the water that night, indeed that whole season of the year, and, our boat's wake left little trails of green fire, as the waves broke into the air. When we got to the shore, we could see the waves coming in to the beach, and every wave's crest had a little line of green fire riding on its' edge, as it came to shore. It was very beautiful, really, and the Iranian people were very hospitable and friendly unto us that whole visit that week. They had warned us to stay out of the red light district, and, I think most of us did, though I could not say for sure. I went into town, and had two beers (Tuborg Gold) and a great steak dinner. After so long at sea, seven weeks, two beers was plenty enough for me, and I went back to the ship, to sleep, a deep sleep, that I had been wanting for a long time.

There was the time, in the Indian Ocean, when the water decided to imitate a huge mirror, and became like a sheet of glass, as far as the eye could see, in all directions. The wake of our ship could be traced out to the horizon, behind us, since it was the only two waves out there. This went on for two days, as we crossed that ocean, toward Africa. I have no idea how vast the huge calm area was, but it was one of the strangest things I ever did see.

There was another time, also in the Indian Ocean, when the natural luminescence of the plankton, or whatever they were, glowed with a soft green light, like a gigantic, endless night light in a kid's room. The ship seemed like this totally dark thing, moving through green milk, an alien intruder into the world of green-milk oceans.

The Indian Ocean seemed in some ways an ocean from a different world, and not just because all the places where we went, there were very strange countries, for an American's traditions. Among all the strange, and most unusual sights that I was privileged to see, was a clear and beautiful night, when I could see the comet Kehoutek with my own eyes. That was one of those nights where you look up, and wonder why all the stars don't run into each other, since you can see just how astonishingly many there are, and how close to each other they seem. It is very obvious why early sailors used the stars for navigation. Whether it's the North Star, above the Equator, or the Southern Cross, if south of the Equator, on a clear night at sea, a sailor always has a perfect visual compass.

Once, I saw an enormous tree, floating upside down in the sea, and the roots were sticking up out of the water forty feet, or so. I wonder just how big the top end of that tree, hidden under water, might have been, and just how much of a monster that storm had been, that could rip loose a whole lumberyard's worth of a tree like that, and just hurl it out to sea.

One time, when we were in the Gulf of Aden, just a few miles off of the coast of Africa, we were caught in a desert dust storm that had blown all the way out to sea. For two days, as we went about our assigned mission, we had to cover all the air intake vents with fine mesh cheesecloth, to keep out the ultra-fine dust. Anyone who went topside had to wear a serious dust mask, and a respirator, if they were to be outside for any length of time, just as though with paint fumes. The sun could not be clearly seen, but was just a brighter spot in the hazy glare. We were very glad to leave that experience behind. Clean sea air never smelled quite so good, as when we cleared that mess.

 As part of what I did, I had to learn about some oceanography, including thermal layers, bottom characteristics, current patterns, and sound propagation patterns, as well as sound shadow zones. These occur when the water suddenly changes to a colder layer, and the sound waves are deflected back upward, instead of continuing straight, since the water, when colder, is denser. In water, temperature is a greater factor affecting density than is increasing pressure, with depth. Colder water is denser, deeper water is not. Deeper water, is, however, always colder, and the sharp boundary bounces back sound waves.

There were occasions when we were raced by many dolphins, all of them pacing alongside our ship, leaping in and out of the water, clearing the water by as much as 8 to 10 feet, and remaining airborne for at least 20 or 30 feet, as they were racing alongside us playfully, at speeds of 35 knots and more, as if they were teasing us, and saying, "Can't you guys get that big thing to go any faster?"

There were strange, living mysteries under the surface, also. Since I was in something to do with Anti Submarine Warfare, I often was near the ship's sonar equipment. The most haunting, otherworldly sounds came in through our sonar receivers, and we heard the deep water whale songs, which are full of meaning, and language, and yet are such complete mysteries to our minds. Very, strangely, beautiful, is the best way to describe that experience.

There was the time that the Captain came on to the ship's intercom, and told us all that we had been good boys, since we had scored extremely well, a few days earlier, in a test we took in Hawaii. He then told us that we were going to go swimming, whereupon, a loud cheer was heard all over the ship! They hung cargo nets down the sides of the ship, and put out a few of the guys in a motor whaleboat, with shark repellent, and high powered rifles, just in case. The boat kept a zone of protection, constantly tracing back and forth, in a half circle, enclosing us on one side, while the ship was our barricade, behind us. On the other side of the ship, some fellows were trying to see if they could do the same sort of thing that I did, as a five year old, but I do not know if they were actually trying to also catch a shark!

The strange sensation in your thoughts is quite unique, when you are actually in the water, and you suddenly remember that if you wanted your toes to touch bottom, you would have to stand three miles tall, to be able to do it. It's as if there is no limit to the water's depth below you, like it continues for infinity. I guess maybe the astronauts feel that way, even more, when they do a space walk. They can actually see all the way down, and so can feel the vast distance even more intensely. Spooky!

There was the time when we went through a typhoon, a big one that lasted four days. We had been in port, but had had to ship out, since the storm could do some serious damage to our ship, if it was slammed against the concrete pier, again and again. By the end of the second day, everyone, and I do mean everyone, was as sea sick as a dog. We staggered to our watch stations, when we had to go stand watch, and tried not to throw up, since we all only had dry heaves left at that point. We couldn't sleep, since the ocean kept trying to turn our 8,000 ton ship upside down, and throwing us out of our racks. Trying to use the head brought out a whole new set of unimaginable terrors to conquer. It got messy in there, and everyone was too sick to clean it up, for two days. Even our rugged Captain went to his cabin, and closed the door. The ship's Doctor ran out of Dramamine, or, seasick pills. For meals, one of the cooks managed to put out Gatorade, and crackers, but almost no one even tried to eat.

Conversely, once when we tied up to a concrete pier in Singapore, as we left the ship, to go out into town, and, of course, find a bar, we noticed that it felt like the whole pier was rolling from side to side, like a ship. Our bodies had gotten so used to the constant roll of the ship at sea, that on solid ground, it took us about two hours before the ground stopped seeming to roll from side to side, and no, we were not drunk, at least, not yet. When you first go to sea, you have to get your sea legs. After a long time at sea, you have to get back your land legs!

When a ship comes into port, all along the side, many crew members are assigned places in the line handling detail. Usually, each division is given the responsibility for one of six main lines. After a few tryouts, one person per group is chosen as the line-heaver. The heaving line is ½ inch cotton rope, with what is called a monkey fist at the end, which is a special, hard knot, very solid. Since I happened to be given a gift for accurate throwing, or maybe because they knew I was from Texas, they made me throw the heaving line. I do not remember which port it was, but they had a lot of ships in port right then. Maybe, it was Subic Bay. Anyway, we had to tie up outboard of another two ships already tied-up, and when we got in position, and were close enough, they told us to tie up. That was my cue, and I threw the line just as I always did. This time it did something very special, and, performing a stunt that no one else I talked to had ever seen, the knot went over the top safety line on the other ship, then looped around, under the second safety line down, and looped back up again, tying itself into a knot! It immediately made me a legend on our ship, and some of the guys actually gave me a standing ovation for it, and some of the sailors on the other ship did, too! I cannot take credit for it. Neither is he that plants anything, nor he that waters, but God, which gives the increase. Also, the lot is cast into the lap, but the whole disposing thereof is of the Lord. The heaving line was cast to the other ship, but when it tied itself into a one in a million knot when it got there, well, then,

Somebody Else, besides me, made that happen.

The full moon on the open ocean is something you ought to see, if you ever get the chance. It is big and bright, as you never see it anywhere else. It makes the whole ocean look very mysterious. If you want to talk, about raw memory material, for future dreams, well, the open ocean in full, bright moonlight is a great mental video, which will stay with you for a lifetime.

One of my most favorite memories of my ocean voyages occurred one fine day, when my ship and another ship were steaming parallel to each other, about 70 yards apart, at about 20 knots, into the wind. Our two ships were linked by a very strong cable, strung tightly, and constantly, automatically kept at the precise correct tension. This is the method by which ships transfer fuel, food, and other things between two ships at sea. It is an underway replenishment transfer, and so is called "Un-rep". Well, one of the other things, sometimes transferred by cable, is people. This day was my day, since my time to go home, to be honorably discharged, had come, at last! They strapped me into a special enclosing safety chair, made of tubular frame work, with lots of straps and such, so I wouldn't be thrown out in rough seas. I was lifted over the side, and hung in mid-air from the cable, between the ships, as we were all moving along at the same speed, in the same direction. I was wildly overjoyed, and it felt like a carnival ride and a life-saving rescue, to freedom, and a new life, back home. I was shouting praise to our good Lord, at least half of the way across, and waving back, smiling at my friends, as I watched my ship fade away in the distance. Maybe that's about the way it looks, when a believer dies and is carried up to Heaven.

Not too much time passed after that, until I saw an even more favorite view of the mighty, endless ocean. It was as we left Hawaii, early in the morning, after refueling our plane. The morning was very heavily overcast, and so humid, you could almost feel the rain about to drip right out of the air as you walked through it. Anyway, as we left the Island, we came up suddenly, through the cloud layers, and our pilot turned our plane eastward, toward Stateside, and home-sweet-home! I happened to be sitting in a window seat, and I also happened, by the grace of our good Lord, to have my 35 millimeter camera with me. I saw what I think was the single most beautiful, breathtaking, and spectacular sunrise that I ever saw in my whole life. Even now, many years, and many thousands of sunrises later, I still cannot match it. The clouds were so ruggedly sculptured, that they appeared as floating, golden mountains, with great peaks, and deep, mysterious valleys. The Sun was shining right between two of the peaks, and blazing along the floor of the great cloud valley, that ran toward my window. I began snapping photos, and got in three, before the pilot made another adjustment, and the view was lost. The best of the three shots I named "Promise", and it is the cover shot on my very first book, "When Light Became A Man".

Maybe my ultimate favorite view of the ocean was when we finally saw San Francisco, as we looked out the window of our plane, while we came in for an afternoon landing. It is impossible to adequately describe just how much you can miss your home, and your family, and your friends. You can never know precisely how it feels, unless you have experienced it. As bad as the time away feels, it feels that much better, once the Lord has brought you home again, all in one piece, if you are that blessed.

So, as you can easily tell, even though 35 years have passed through my own life, since I was last on the open ocean, a part of it came on shore with me. The old expression is something like "having saltwater in your veins" but it is still a real phenomenon, none the less. A sailor may leave the ocean, but the ocean never leaves the sailor.

I have saved the best, for last. The most beautiful thing which I ever saw, while I lived on the ocean, was nothing physical. It was the greatness, the vastness, the endlessness, the beauty, the majesty, and the living power and presence of Almighty God. I was allowed to begin to get to know our good Lord, in ways I never would have, if I had not sailed where I did. They say that there are no atheists in the foxhole. That is likely true. I also think that most of the fellows that spend any time on the ocean also are changed, and their faith is increased and strengthened. I met some sailors with dead souls, but, certainly, you run into zombies at the grocery store, and everywhere you go. I also was very privileged to serve with some of the finest, bravest, and most intensely Christian men I ever knew in my life. Every one of them agreed with me, that our lives, and our faith, had been improved forever, since we were blessed to live as sailors, for a time, in our journey.

When we went out into the vast unknown of the ocean, Jesus Christ, our Savior, was also a great Sailor, and was already there, waiting to meet with us! I am looking forward to meeting some of those shipmates again soon, in a place where the streets are paved with gold. Those of us, who love Jesus, have already chosen the Captain under which we will sail, because He first invited us to join His crew. Besides, what better Captain could there be, than the One Who made the oceans? Remember, they have to calm down, and be still, whenever He tells them to do so.

TIRED ENOUGH TO SLEEP THROUGH A STORM

This was not the first time a prophet of Almighty God had been in this type of situation. Many centuries earlier, another prophet, named Jonah, had also been asleep in a storm tossed ship. The power of the storm had been about to rip the ship into pieces, and some of the crew members had found Jonah, exhausted, asleep in the lower part of the ship. They had awakened him in distress, insisting that he arise and pray to whatever God he trusted, if perhaps they might be spared, at least their lives, if not the ship's cargo.

This time, the prophet was the King of Prophets, Jesus Christ, and He was asleep in the stern of the fishing ship, within which He and His twelve disciples were crossing a very stormy sea. These fishing vessels were extremely sea-worthy, or the men would have stopped using them, since the Sea of Galilee was often stormy. This storm had developed suddenly, like a spring tornado in Texas, and was severe enough that a dozen fit, experienced crewmen were losing the battle to keep the water out of the ship. Those ships had very high sides, but 20-foot tall waves were able to dump a lot of water into the boat every few seconds. The crew sailing with Jesus that day also went and woke Him up, asking Him to somehow save their lives, and maybe the ship, too.

    Jonah and his shipmates calmed the angry sea by throwing Jonah into the sea, whereupon God made the waters calm down, and all the men that remained on board humbled themselves before God, and worshipped and obeyed Him, and prayed that they might not be charged with the innocent blood of Jonah. As it turned out later, Jonah did actually survive, and that prayer was granted to those sailors. The noble part of that is that Jonah told them to throw him into the sea, since he knew that the storm was because of his disobedience unto God. His willing self-sacrifice made the salvation of the crew, and even the whole ship, possible.

Jesus Christ did not have to pray about it, or ask Almighty God to calm the storm, or save the crew, or forgive His disobedience. Jesus Christ is Almighty God, and He never disobeyed, and He came indeed to save the crew, and the ship, so He just stood up, and directly ordered the wind and the water to sit down, and shut up, and they immediately did just that. The noble part about that is that He came with the primary purpose of willingly self-sacrificing His life for all of us who believe in Him, not just for His crew of twelve.

Both times the storm calmed, and both times it was a true, anointed Prophet of God that calmed the storm, and saved the crew, and the ship, too. Both times, it eventually required the prophet to give a willing self-sacrifice to achieve it, even if, in the case of Jesus Christ, He still was scheduled to work many more miracles, and preach many more sermons, and teach many more parables, before the sacrifice was finalized.

Both times, the men of each crew were spared, saving not only their lives in this world, but also they all had their hearts turned seriously unto God, resulting in changed, obedient lives, and thankful, humble hearts.

Another common feature was that, both times, the prophet lived beyond his, or His, self-sacrifice, although, in the case of Jesus Christ, it did require Him to be resurrected to resume living. Both of the prophets also saved all of their fellow crew members. They both saved many more people, in addition. Each prophet saved an entire people from being destroyed.

Also, Jesus Himself referred to Jonah, saying that even as Jonah was three days and three nights in the belly of the great fish, so also the Son of Man (Jesus) would be three days and three nights in the belly of the Earth. He said that that similar miracle, a return to life, after three days and nights, would be the only sign given unto that generation.

He also mentioned Jonah by recalling how the people of Nineveh had repented at the preaching of Jonah, and a greater than Jonah was there (referring unto Himself).

When Jesus Christ first met Peter, He said, "Your name is Simon, son of Jonah. Henceforth, you shall be called Cephas." The modern English form of Cephas is Peter.

While we do not know if Peter was an actual genetic descendent of the prophet Jonah, or not, we do know that he also later did some very powerful preaching, like at the Day of Pentecost, and when visiting Cornelius, and the books, which Peter wrote, are full of mighty prophecies, indeed. He also was known for a fiery temper, and a brash, impetuous personality. That sounds a lot like Jonah, too. He also was known for his rock-like faith in our good Lord, as was Jonah.

When our Lord was here, He often times referred to earlier prophets, but He mentions Jonah at least three times, and in direct connection with what He declared would be the only sign that He would give unto that generation. Also, He mentioned Jonah in direct connection to preaching and repentance, which was His Own specialty. Also, Jonah was the prophet that also had to be willing to give his own life to save his friends. The magnitude, and significance, of all these common points and patterns is almost overwhelming to contemplate, when they are finally perceived, clearly. It is not certain, precisely, why Jonah and his life were so arranged, to be such a pattern preview of what King Jesus would do, when He arrived.

One thing is evident. Our good Lord thought very highly of Jonah, and, when He called Peter the son of Jonah, it was a very great compliment, whether genetically precise, or not.

Another thing we know is that both prophets started out in luxurious settings, Jonah in the court of the king of Israel, and Jesus in Heaven, with the Father. Each prophet had to leave the comfortable surroundings, and endure an unbelievably difficult, painful, and thankless ordeal, in order to save people, that clearly were not worth saving. Even with all of that, both prophets successfully completed the mission assigned to them by Almighty God. By their obedience, and patience, each one made a real difference for other people, and saved more lives than can be counted.

THE MUSTARD PRINCIPLE

When Jesus was describing metaphors and similes for the Kingdom of Heaven, to try to impart a mental picture of its' very nature, He chose things with which the disciples were familiar. One of the things which He enlisted was the grain of mustard seed, which, when planted, is the least of all seeds, but, when it is grown, is a mighty bush, more like a tree, so big and strong, that birds of the air come and build nests in it, just like an oak tree.

I still remember the day that my Dad, who came from a long line of preachers, warriors, and farmers, showed me a few little grains of mustard seed, while we were out in our backyard, planting our garden. I was only about four, and really was not much of a great garden worker, yet, but Dad still had begun to show me all the fundamentals. Anyway, the seeds looked like a bit of yellow dust, and blew away right out of his palm, when the breeze stirred. I recall a thought that those things were too small to make much of a plant. Later, after a few months, I was proven wrong.

When the good Lord said, "Be LIGHT!!!" the light started out at a single point in space and time, Point Zero, and rapidly spread out into the still-expanding, and even faster expanding, all the time, created thing that we call reality. In terms of size and scope, and also, complexity, that initial blast of light at Point Zero has continued to expand, grow, and modify into various new, interesting, and complex structures, for instance, the human body. Even the pattern of Creation, as a whole, is following the "Mustard Principle".

A fine visual parallel is a pebble dropped into a pond, and the resulting outwardly spreading ripples. If the pond were big enough, the ripples could go on forever, but would eventually fade, as energy was slowly lost through dispersion, by expansion.

Another example is Adam, and Eve, who were told to be fruitful, and multiply, and fill the Earth. Well, that command has certainly been fulfilled.

Another example is Noah, and his family. From that one group, of eight people, came every person alive ever since.

Also, the animals on the Ark, which repopulated the Earth with beasts, present another obvious tie-in.

Another example is Abraham. God changed his name to "Father of Many Nations" and then brought it into reality, over the centuries that followed.

Jacob's name was changed to "Israel" and the promise that was made, was also kept, that in Israel, all the families of the Earth would be blessed. This is certifiably true, since the Savior of all the redeemed people, of mankind, Jesus

Christ, was given to the Earth through Israel.

Perhaps the ultimate example of the Mustard Principle is the good Lord Jesus Christ, Himself. He started out as a single planted seed, sent to bear witness of the truth, and grew and became mighty, and has begun to fill the Earth. God says in the Scripture that He fills Heaven and Earth. One of the ways in which He is doing that is through the Holy Spirit, as more and more people enter into the mystery, and begin to follow Jesus.

In America, we usually think of mustard as a yellow smear on our hotdogs at the ball game. There is more to it than that. Yes, it does add just the perfect flavor enhancement to a hotdog, or a corn-dog, or a turkey sandwich, or maybe a hamburger. It also contains cumin, a powerful anti inflammatory medicine, which has been known, used, and highly valued for centuries, for treatment of arthritis and other body aches and pains. It's not just a condiment.

I do think, that most folks would agree, that since Jesus Christ entered this Earth, things do have a richer, more delightful flavor. I think it can also be observed, that even if there are still aches and pains with us in this world, much help arrives, to bear them better, once you realize that Some One is right there with you, helping you to carry through, until your mission is done.

John the Baptist said that it was time for him to decrease, but for Jesus Christ to increase. In the prophecy of Jesus Christ, in the Book of Revelation, He shows John the Apostle a vision of a great mountain, which grew, and grew, until it filled the entire Earth. This is usually understood to be the Earth during the Millennium, as the Kingdom of Heaven rebuilds the whole world. It could also equally portray the expansion of the body of Christ, during this current age, as the Holy Spirit causes the church, worldwide, to grow and deepen.

It is likely that Jesus gave us the Mustard Principle, as the most appropriate and streamlined analogy, of which He could think, to show us a core insight into the Way that God does almost everything. The Bible declares that neither is he that plants anything, nor he that waters, but God, which gives the increase. It brings God glory, for Him to take a small thing, and make it great, and make it to bear much good fruit. I find this greatly encouraging, since maybe He can take my feeble attempts to properly thank and honor Him, and maybe make them grow into something a little bit bigger, and better, I hope. That Way, He gets the glory, but I get the contentment, of my mission completed. That is worth a lot, to me.

THE CORRECT PATTERN

There was a time, in Israel, when there was no king in the land, and every man did what was right in his own eyes. (The Word of God declares that every way of a man is right in his own eyes, but the Lord weighs the hearts.) As would seem obvious, that kingless era in Israel, the time of the judges, was a wild and wooly time, something which made the old "wild west" in America look like kindergarten, by comparison. It was not only individuals, and small groups, that did bizarre and destructive things (horrid atrocities which would make 21st century Americans recoil with revulsion). It was also entire tribes, and nations, and alliances of nations, which committed unspeakable terrors, often upon weaker, helpless victims. As if all of that were not enough, a group of cousins to the Greeks, the Philistines, had decided that they wanted to own this land flowing with milk and honey, and were following the Egyptian road to extreme self-destruction, and were trying to exterminate the Hebrews. The God of Israel was not going to tolerate that.

There were a couple of Hebrew folks, that loved the Lord, and obeyed Him, and wanted to have a child, but were entering middle age, and had not yet been given the gracious gift of a baby. They prayed that God might grant them a child. One day the woman was out in the field, picking things to cook for supper, and a strange man appeared before her, suddenly! She was startled, but he reassured her to not worry, because he had been sent to tell her that she would soon have a son. The parents were to call his name Samson, and no razor was to ever touch his hair, because he was to be a Nazirite unto the Lord from even before his birth. It was promised that Samson would begin to deliver Israel from the cruel oppression of the Philistines, which he, later, did fulfill.

The woman was stunned, then overjoyed, and wanted to share the good news with her husband, so she asked the strange man to wait a few moments, while she went into the house to fetch him. He agreed. A few minutes later, they both were running back to the man, wildly excited, and out of breath with joy. After the husband confirmed his understanding of the details of the message, he wished to make a thanksgiving sacrifice, and asked the stranger to stay while he prepared it. The unusual man agreed, but said he would not partake of it himself. He told the husband to make the altar, in the "correct pattern", and then offer the sacrifice upon it.

The man busied himself for some time, laying out the necessary twelve un-carved stones, first, in two interlocking triangles, and then, wherever strings crossed between each stone, another inner stone, six more total, for a grand total of twelve. About two hundred years later, a king, named David, would use this same ancient, holy pattern, the interlocking two triangles, that the world has come to know as the Star of David. Every time a flag of Israel is seen, that same pattern is shown. David was a man after God's own heart. No wonder that King David chose that "correct pattern" for his royal symbol. His whole life was lived upon the altar, for God.

The special symbolism, of two interlocking triangles, is fairly straightforward. One triangle is pointing upward, the other downward, but both are equal, and they form a coherent total pattern, in combination. The three vertices of each triangle correspond directly to Father, Savior, and Holy Spirit. The sides of the triangles correspond to the permanent, intimate bond that forever exists between God in

His manifestation as Father, and God, in His manifestation as Savior, and God, in His manifestation as Holy Spirit. The triangle pointing upward is because He is Lord of Heaven, and the triangle pointing downward is because He is Lord of Earth.

The holy, secret pattern had first been ordained by Moses and Aaron. It was the "correct pattern" they used, when building altars in the wilderness. It was the "correct pattern" Joshua used, when the waters of the Jordan River were stopped, so all of Israel could walk into the Promised Land, on dry ground, as their fathers had crossed the Gulf of Aquba, on dry ground, between the walls of seawater on each side. Few people seem to realize that this illustrates yet another of God's holy patterns. When Abraham went up on to Mount Moriah (the Temple Mount, today) to sacrifice Isaac, after he was stopped by God, he sacrificed a ram, instead. At that time,

Abraham was led, by God, to walk between the halves of the sacrifice, just as, later, his descendents would walk between the waters, and not be dunked under them. The ones that got dunked were the evil Egyptians.

God does certain things, certain ways, for certain reasons, and He does not like it much, when people try to change the way that He wants it done. It is better, even if we do not understand, to just go ahead and obey Him, and trust that He knows why He wants it that way, even if we don't. For example, remember the uncarved, or unshaped, stones. God specified it that way, because He said, "Do not swing your blade upon it, for when you swing your tool upon it, you defile it." He understands that, whether we do, or not.

Well, the man completed his preparations, and lit the fire to complete the sacrifice. The unusual stranger, whose face was beautiful and terrible, a wonder, and a fearful thing to behold, looked at them, and smiled, and jumped right up into the roaring flames of the bonfire, and flew straight up to Heaven!

THE FIRST RAINDROP

Although the night was clear, and supernaturally calm, it was just before a silent storm opened warfare in the darkness. It was the new moon, and pitch black everywhere, except for brilliant starlight, which does not much help in finding steady pathways at night.

Noah and his wife, and their three sons, and their wives, were all soundly asleep, on board the Ark, all of them in their special upper deck cabins. Noah's dreams were sometimes troubled, this night, with vague unease about something, or other. He tossed and turned, but kept trying to roll over, and get some sleep, since the Lord had told him that tomorrow would be a special day.

All around the Ark, the animals had gathered into their groups and families, and were soundly resting, at peace. None of the humans or animals knew that a hellish horde of evil men and twisted animals, led by demons, was sneaking closer every minute. There were others that were watching, some that would not allow harm to even ruffle one of the feathers on one of the chickens, which were sleeping calmly, next to the foxes and coyotes.

In the War Room of Heaven, King Jesus watched the situation develop, along with His little brothers, King Adam, and Prince Abel, and Prince Seth, and all of the other righteous ancestors of Noah, including Enoch, whose death had been reserved for the last few days of Earth. Methuselah had also just arrived, since he had died that morning, and had been buried by Noah and his sons that afternoon. Now they all watched intently, with nothing hidden from their eyes, and King Jesus spoke after a few seconds' thought. He said, "Adam, send your hunters now, to kill and drive away the dinosaurs. Tell them to drag the enemy corpses away before daylight, after they finish killing them."

Adam smiled, a truly happy, excited smile, and sent out a shrill, piercing blast of a whistle. Wolf and She-wolf came bounding into the War Room, which stood upon the deck of the Throne Room of Heaven (but the War Room had no walls, since Heaven did not keep secrets from the people there). As they came up, all tail-wagging, and eager, Adam gave them their orders, and said, "Get 'em!" The two gigantic wolves instantly leapt into the air, and flew straight down to Earth, to launch the counter attack against the dinosaurs. They each knew that they were more than a match for even the T-rexes, and could toss even Brontosaurs through the air with ease.

King Jesus smiled, as He watched them leap to the battle. Then, He turned to Tzedek-el, the General of the Earth-assigned portion of the Army of Heaven, the ground troops, and told him, "Okay, time to get back down there to your angels, and chase down, arrest, and bind those demons, so we can get them out of the fight right now. The evil humans will lose their courage and resolve, once you have rounded up the enemy angels. Go!" The angel General vanished, launching instantaneously into the fight with his part of the army.

King Jesus then turned to the men in Heaven with Him, the ten that were Noah's ancestors, and also Prince Abel. He smiled again, this time a very scary smile, and said, "Okay, little brothers. Grab your swords, and follow Me! We're going to kill a few evil humans tonight, for even daring to threaten Noah, and the rest of Our Family. I would kill them anyway, for bothering the good animals, but why should we stay here, and let the wolves and angels have all of the fun? Let's go!"

When He said that, all of them took flight, on great, glorious, powerful wings! With drawn, blazing swords of Justice and Holiness, they flew like living arrows of fire into the thick of the fight, roaring "HOLY! HOLY! HOLY!"

Every one of the evil creatures saw them all coming, glowing with the Holy Fire of God in the black night! The mob of evil had counted on no resistance, and helpless, sleeping victims, and had no heart for a real fight. They turned, and ran, flew, or slithered away, as fast as they could. It did none of them any good. The screams of the dying monsters would have shaken concrete walls, and would have waked the people and animals near the Ark, if King Jesus had not intercepted them, many miles away. Wolf, and She-wolf, both over twelve feet tall, when sitting, had made bloody, quick work of killing over a thousand carnivorous dinosaurs, in less than an hour. The angel General, Tzedek-el, and his army of

100,000 angels, had finished grabbing and binding all of the several thousand evil angels, in less than seven minutes total.

It took a little longer for King Jesus and the rest of Heaven's Royal Household to finish killing the evil humans. Their grim task lasted almost three hours, but there were only a dozen humans doing the killing, and they had about six thousand evil humans to exterminate. When they were finished, they were not even tired, and their flaming swords were still clean, and their white robes and armor were still unsmeared with blood. Every drop of blood they had shed that holy night had been only evil blood, and so it could not stain them at all.

As Wolf and She-wolf returned from removing the last of the corpses (into a deep crack in the Earth, where they could finish rotting, until the Flood came and hid them) the King of Kings raised His

Hand, and shouted, "Well done! Now, let's get back to Heaven, before the Sun rises!" The moment He finished speaking, everyone, men, angels, and wolves, rose, in a flash, and disappeared into the pre-dawn sky, streaking light trails behind them, as they returned Home.

Noah snorted in his sleep, and, finally giving up on sleeping any more this night, rolled out of bed, and climbed up to the top weather deck, to see what kind of morning it would be, and to start his day with the Lord, in prayer. As he stood up outside, he saw what he thought were dim clouds on the distant horizon, which were hard to see in the morning twilight, while the stars were still out. He thanked, and blessed the good Lord, and then asked, "About how much longer, Lord?" As he looked up to the sky, while still asking the question, a single drop of water fell from the sky, and landed right on Noah's nose, right at the tip! Noah laughed out loud, and said, "Okay, Lord! I better get those boys of mine up, so we can get the animals on board, right now! We'll have to make breakfast later on, I guess." Noah turned, and went down the ladder, to obey the good Lord, and to help to save the world.

THE FIRST NAVAL WAR

They had been at sea for about four months. The enormous, world wide waves had finally subsided, and, most of the time, the ocean surface was more of a series of calm, large swells, with slow, wide, rolling troughs. The weather had turned beautiful, as the storm clouds had cleared away, and clean, ultra-fresh air greeted them everywhere they sailed, and it always smelled like salt. (Sailed was actually not the correct term, in modern connotations, since the Ark had no sails, and was driven by wind and current patterns, wherever Almighty God, in His infinite Wisdom, decided it should go.)

All of the people and animals were holding up very nicely, although every creature on board longed for dry, solid ground again, and the sight and smell of something alive and green, besides seaweed and kelp. There were plenty enough dried food provisions stored on board, in special places along the outer bulkheads of the ark, just inside the planks of gopher wood. They had carefully pitched the hull of the Ark, for over twenty years, to waterproof it, but, if it sprang a leak, (because it could hit a rock, or a floating large tree, or maybe an iceberg) then the grains stored along the outer bulkheads should swell up when wet, and either stop, or at least, slow down, any leaks that developed.

    Noah and his sons had no idea at all where they were on the Earth, except that they were at sea. They were always at sea. They never even saw any land, or much of anything else, except for unlimited ocean, and unlimited sky, without exception. Sometimes it was hot, sometimes it was cold, sometimes it was stormy, and sometimes it became very calm. Everybody was adjusting very well, and everybody kept very busy, feeding, walking, and tending all the animals, as well as cleaning out their pens, and putting in fresh straw, of which they had stored many tons, all over the Ark. For a fresh food supply, God had given them an ocean full of fresh fish, but instructed them to catch and eat the types that were safe to eat raw, since it would have been unthinkable to kindle a fire upon a wooden vessel, at least, not until insulated steel ovens were invented. For the most part, every one ate grains and nuts, and a bunch of sun dried fruit which they had prepared, as well. Noah and his family ran laps around the top deck, too, when the seas were calm enough to do so safely. They had long ropes, if anyone should fall over board, and the Ark was not a self-powered vessel, so, it did not move very fast, in relation to the water around it. If someone had fallen in, he would have been able to slowly swim alongside long enough for the others to rescue him, and they had several ropes already hanging down the sides, all around. This was a prudent, fore-thought safety measure, since the sides of the Ark towered up out of the water over twenty feet, with almost thirty feet of ship below the waterline. The extra ballast, provided by hundred of tons of animals, was just precisely perfect, to give the optimum stability to the vessel, no matter how rough the sea state became. It rode like a big, slow island, most of the time. (Modern aircraft carriers are about that size, and rough seas do not usually bother them much, either.)

Noah had forbidden anyone to go topside after sunset, or before dawn, since it was just too dangerous. One night, when they were all fast asleep, rocked gently by the long, slow swells, a lone attacker began a submarine attack against the Ark, and its' passengers.

The thing which had once been a cherub, and had originally started out with much, much more power, and ability, had been reduced to a greatly diminished thing, and now had no more beauty, but was revealed as the ugly dragon that had hidden within its' evil, dead heart. (As he thought in his heart, so is he.) After the Flood, and the failed attack, in a vain attempt to destroy the Ark, even before the Flood, the dragon had been nursing its' wounds, which had been dealt unto it by Michael, the War Cherub. It still was a supernatural thing, and had hidden way down deep, in the bottom most part of the ocean, in the Mariana's Trench, near the modern island of Guam. (Of course, the good Lord still saw it, and knew right where it was, all the time. God had never let His attention wander away from the monster, ever since it had killed Eve.) God had decided to let it alone, for now, as long as it stayed out of the Way, of what He was going to do, no matter what.

    This night, the dragon stirred, and began a rapid ascent, up from what would normally have been a seven mile depth. It was deeper now, with the current Flood conditions. The serpent knew where the Ark was, of course, and made a torpedo streak toward it, although it was about a half a world away, when he started. If he had still had the full power of a cherub, he could have been there in less than an eye blink, by passing through the water as though it did not exist. Now, he had to do things the harder way, and feel the resistance of the medium, as he passed through it. Even so, nothing less than the dragon, or any of the three good cherubs, would have had the strength or ability to make such a great swim. Good angels would not have felt any resistance, but bad angels would not have had the strength to make it.

As he sped toward his target, he left behind a boiling mess in the depths, and produced a glowing streak over ten miles wide, where the force of his passage actually heated the water enough to make it boil, and vaporize, and even glow a dull yellow-orange from the extraordinary heat he generated, even miles below the surface, in near-freezing water. His rate of travel was in the hundreds of knots, and even modern weapons of men could not have kept up with him, or fought against him, at all. As he traveled, he occasionally veered a little off course, to snag an entire whale, or giant squid, along the way, swallowing them whole. He did not need to eat, but he did love to kill all of God's creatures, no matter what. He loved to cause needless terror, pain, suffering, and death. As long as someone else, besides himself, was feeling the pain, he delighted in watching it.

    The damn dragon was still a huge creature. In his original form, he could have stood upon Earth, and his head would have been in space. Now, he was much smaller, and weaker, but he was still bigger than anything else in the ocean. He began, in his own grotesque way, to sort of salivate, with the kind of deadly venom that only a dragon of evil could generate. As droplets of it trailed behind him, it killed instantly, if any living thing touched it.

The enemy did not need to use sonar ranging, as do dolphins and whales. He could actually see through the few miles of sea remaining, until he hit his impact point. Even in the pitch black, the Ark glowed in the dark, bright with the souls of living things, which he intended snuffing out, in a few more seconds. He opened his mammoth jaws wide enough to swallow the entire Ark, and everything on it.

Suddenly, he stopped moving forward! Strain as he might, using his wings as giant flippers, he churned the water to a storm of chaos. Still, he could not move forward. In rage, he screamed his anger into the sea.

As his ear-splitting scream faded, he heard a deep voice behind him, laughing richly. He looked over his shoulder, and saw a dazzling light in the water, which made his eyes squint. As he blinked against the glare, he could make out the cherub, Michael, calmly holding on to his tail, keeping him motionless, with just one huge hand!

Panic set in, and the enemy, although made without fear, originally, had been given the ability to feel fear, and, at moments like this, stark, raving terror! He began to struggle, uselessly, as Michael dragged him away, back toward the Mariana's Trench. He started trying to scream curses at Michael, until Michael calmly told him, "You shall be silent now. The Lord rebukes you!" After that, the dragon could not speak any more, all the way back to the trench, which only took a few seconds, since Michael could ignore the water resistance, and whatever he carried with him went where he took it. He was the ultimate marshal.

Michael took the enemy down to the depths, and chained him there for a time, with a great, unbreakable, supernatural Chain of Justice, forged by King Jesus, Himself. As he left the dragon there in the cold, pitch black, deepest part of the ocean, he turned a moment to say, "The King says you are to stay put for now. So, you will. We will meet again, someday. Next time, I will not be so gentle with you, worm!"

Back on the Ark, one of Noah's dreams showed him a vision of a future grandchild of his, one of Shem's, a small child named Elam. The child, in the dream, ran up to Noah, and jumped up into his lap, and said that he had had a bad dream, about a terrible monster. Noah had smiled, and chuckled gently, then said, "Yes, boy, that would be the dragon. You do not need to worry about him, any more. The good Lord watches over our people, and the dragon is no match for Him!"

BLESS GOD, AMERICA

Bless God, America!

He shows us His love!

He stands beside us, to guide us,

Through the night, with His light, from above.

He made the mountains, and the valleys, and the oceans,

White with foam!

Bless God, America! He gave us our home!

Bless God, America! He gave us our home!

THE CONVERT

He only vaguely remembered the first time he had ever seen the fellow. It was almost twenty one years ago, and the boy had just turned twelve. For three straight days, beginning every day at sunrise, the boy had come to Solomon's Porch, in the Hebrew Temple, and had asked questions that none of the high priests, or any of the scribes, could fully answer. Oddly enough, the boy knew the answers, which He revealed unto the puzzled adults, once they gave up trying to guess, and just asked Him to tell them the answer. They were frantically opening and closing scroll after scroll of the Scriptures, trying to keep up with Him, and to respond to His machine-gun-like question and answer session. When He was speaking, every one of the adults held silence, hungry to hear what new mysteries that He would spring forth. It was strange, indeed, to watch a mere lad instruct, and intellectually humble, the most educated, and sharpest minds in all of Israel, especially in matters of the Law and the Prophets. When He expounded point after point to them, He always quoted the precise Scripture which He wished to use as a reference, and his quotations were flawlessly perfect! He even spoke unto them in ancient Hebrew, which only the High Priests and the Sanhedrin usually even bothered to learn. The scribes all knew it also, of course, since the ancient Scripture was not written in Aramaic. There was no logical natural reason why a child would know or understand that language, hundreds of years after it fell into disuse, but He still did, and He spoke it without error, even pronouncing the ancient words in the ancient dialect and accent. Moses and David would have understood His Words, but the Maccabees might not have made much sense of them. Abraham would have also understood, but modern Jews, and those carried away to Babylon would have had problems.

As Nicodemus listened and watched, occasionally asking a question, or two, himself, he was perhaps the most stunned one of all of them. He had just been made the Chief Scribe of Israel, only a year before, by unanimous vote of the rest of the Sanhedrin. Now, he was the one to whom they came for precise information from the Scripture, concerning any confusing matter of the Law. He was, in effect, the Chief Justice of their Supreme Court, and his word was final, with the full weight of the Law on his side, in any disputed issue of the Law.

There was an odd moment, on the third afternoon, just before the ninth hour, the hour of prayer, at three o'clock. All of the adult priests had fallen silent, worn out over the last three days, trying vainly to out-riddle Him. Now, they were just listening, very intently, and thoughtfully, deeply digesting the strange and very heavy concepts which He was revealing unto them. He had paused for a moment, after finishing His latest explanation, and suddenly looked over at Nicodemus, and smiled, like a glorious sunrise. He said, "You will see me again, Friend, and then you will remember what things you saw and heard here. You will ask Me again, about the mysteries of Heaven, and I will tell you more, then. I am telling you this, now, long before it comes to pass, that when it does come to pass, you may believe!"

As He finished the last Word, His parents suddenly arrived, as a concerned, but calm, Dad, and a concerned, but much less calm, Mom. His mother scolded Him sharply, and demanded an explanation as to why He had dealt so with them. He had smiled, slightly, and said, calmly, "Did you not know that I must be about My Father's business?" This answer immediately silenced Mary, since she knew, very well, to which Father He was referring. He returned home quietly with them, and never got into any other trouble in His life. Technically, He was the One that had been right this time, too, although his parents did not see that point of view, not until years later.

These days, not too many were still around from that time, and the boy was now a grown, and powerful Man. He was physically rugged, as one could expect from a Man that spent His entire youth doing extreme hard work as a carpenter, in a time when the only power for power tools came from human muscles. He was also a mountain climber, and that had been His favorite pastime, and every Sabbath, after worship, He climbed all afternoon, and came back by sunset, to finish the day of rest. In those days, climbers did not have climbing equipment, except for hands, feet, muscles, and a sharp mind to pick only safe handholds and foot perches. Most folks in those days thought mountain climbers were crazy, and since climbers did not have climbing equipment, they were correct to think that, at least, climbers certainly were adventurous.

The Man had such a vital presence, that whenever He commanded a paralyzed man to stand up and walk, the guy obeyed. When He told someone they could see again, they did. When He told dead people to get up and start living again, they did. The Man inspired confidence and faith. That was precisely what He was trying to do.

It was not until the Monday morning before Passover, that the conflict between the unbelievers on the Sanhedrin, and the newly-revealed Prophet, came to an explosive collision. As long as He had stayed out in the small towns, and villages, the Sanhedrin had been content to let Him alone. But now, He had come charging into the Temple, and physically kicked out several dozen merchants from the courtyard of the temple, and forbidden them to defile the Holy Temple with such things ever again. Since the members of the Sanhedrin had a huge percentage of the animal sales that occurred there, this amounted to hitting them right in the pocketbook. Maybe they might overlook anything else, but, since they loved money so much, instead of God, they decided they had to stop Him, now.

As they gathered in the inner rooms, to plot against Him, they accused Him of much, and defamed Him with being a Law-breaker, just because He was hurting their bottom line of profits. They were more concerned about profits, than prophets.

Nicodemus listened, with growing outrage at the other members of the council. At last, when he could listen to no more, he shouted, "Does our Law condemn a Man before it hears Him?"

This had the effect of detonating a legal nuclear bomb right in the middle of their plots. As the council members fell silent, they realized what he had just done. When it came to a final decision vote, six members of the council voted first, openly, with no secret ballot, and then Nicodemus, as Chief Scribe, cast the final vote, which often was the tie-breaker. But, equally important, he had the right to throw out any case that was not brought to trial correctly, according to actual Law, not just a hot-headed hasty decision, nor a frame-up. If prescribed protocol was not adhered unto, the case could be declared invalid, and the only man who had that decision, in all of Israel, was Nicodemus. He could only be over-ruled by a full six-vote majority against him, and his friend, Joseph of Arimathea, always voted with him, and had for many years. Joseph was also very powerful, since he was the Chief Treasurer, and, he had the authority to allocate funds, or withhold them, for any function, or any purpose, as long as Nicodemus said it was Lawful, in that particular case. Together, they made a formidable team, and the other five members often had to cut deals with them, to even try to push their own agendas. Joseph was also the only other council member that had begun to wonder, in private, if this Jesus fellow might indeed be the actual Son of God. Nicodemus and he had discussed this much, in these last three years, as they heard strange stories from all over Israel, and Samaria, too, through the merchants with whom Joseph dealt. Who else could work such astonishing miracles, very well witnessed, by thousands and thousands of people, unless the Man was really the Person that He claimed to be? The only logical explanation, unto a clear-headed thinker, was that this Jesus fellow was really the Messiah. Nonetheless, they both kept it quiet, since they had positions of enormous power and wealth, and were mighty, even among the other council men. No one in all of Israel was more powerful than the council, except, in some things, the High Priest, and in other cases, the king. No one else was any richer, either. The job of council member paid very, very well, in old Jerusalem.

After a few heart-pounding seconds, as the echo of the shout from Nicodemus faded away, down the long marble hallways, the High Priest, Caiaphas, snapped back in fury, "Are you also from Galilee? Search the scripture and see, for no prophet arises out of GALILEE!" He actually screamed the last word, with a purple face, and spit flying out of his mouth. Shaking with rage, and frustration, since he knew he could go no further, he stomped away. He saw that he could not bring Jesus to trial without some sort of evidence of Law-breaking to use against Him.

Later that evening, about an hour after dark, Nicodemus went to the outskirts of Jerusalem, to Bethany, where he knew Jesus was staying with Lazarus. They spoke together for a long time, hours, and Jesus opened many wonderful mysteries to the understanding of Nicodemus. As the time was drawing to a close, and Nicodemus was walking toward the door, to go home, and dream strange dreams, about all he had been shown, Jesus said his name, softly.

Nicodemus stopped walking, and turned around, and looked Jesus in the eyes. Jesus smiled, and said, "I told you I would see you again one day, and today is that day. Do you remember, now?"

As Jesus said the last word, all of the full memory of that amazing event came flooding back into the present consciousness of Nicodemus's mind, and he saw and heard it all as if it had happened that same day. Tears filled his eyes, and he fell to his knees, saying, "I remember! Oh, Lord, I do believe! You are the Holy Son of God!"

He felt the mighty hands of his Lord upon his shoulders, and instantly felt calm joy, as Jesus lifted him up to his feet again, and hugged him, with a strong squeeze, and two seconds later, pushed him back to arm's length, still holding his shoulders, and looked him in the eyes, and said, "I told you then, so you could believe, now. I am glad to see you again, old friend. That is how all the prophecies I have ever sent or spoken will always work. You will hear it first, and then later, when it does come to pass, you will believe!"

Nicodemus took a couple of deep breaths, as Jesus walked him, arm around shoulder, brothers of Heaven together, toward the door. Jesus spoke again, "Now, before you go home tonight, go to the house of Joseph, and tell him what you have seen and heard, both today, and all those years ago. Pray with him, for the

Father to quicken your hearts, so that you may both be born again of Him. Joseph will hear, and since he knows you have never lied to him, he will also believe, through your witness. Then watch and pray, the rest of this week, but do not interfere with what the Father works out these days, no matter how it appears, at the time. On Friday afternoon, both of you be at the governor's, just after the ninth hour, and demand from him My Body, and bury Me. After that, I will see you again, a few days later!"

IT'S A TRAP!

Everything seemed just a little too easy. All they had to do was storm down the same road that had just been used by the Hebrews. They could see them a few miles ahead, as the slowest members of the people of Israel were only now reaching the far side of the miraculously dry floor of the Gulf of Aquba, which is the right arm of the Red Sea. The older and weaker members of the nation were still guarded, escorted, and helped along by the strong young men among the people.

As the Egyptian commander and his army looked down into the strange passageway, they had strong misgivings to overcome. How could water just stand up into two solid, motionless walls, over fifty feet high, and remain in place, as if held back by gigantic sheets of glass, fifty feet high, but over ten miles long?

The Egyptians were not ignorant of supernatural things, since they had, for thousands of years, been practicing dark rituals, kept secret, upon pain of being chosen as the next sacrifice. The policy was silence, or death. The terrifying part of it was that they all knew that the cause of death was that the Egyptian embalmers and mummy makers surgically prepared the victim for ritual burial, including saving their internal organs in clay jars. The terror was that they did it while the victim was still very much alive, and awake. That much needless cruelty was considered necessary by the dark magicians among the Egyptians, since they thought it helped to persuade the devil to aid their cause against their enemies. If Moses had not had his own staff turn into a snake which devoured the magicians' snakes, Egyptians might have kept on thinking that their evil sorcery was the strongest supernatural thing in the world. After a devastating series of plagues and disasters had been sent against Egypt, by God, through Moses, the Egyptians were not as hasty to disregard the supernatural things of Moses and Israel, not these days.

There were some of Pharaoh's magicians along for the battle, or, as Pharaoh expected, the slaughter. The commander called them to his chariot, and demanded signs from them, as to whether it was safe to proceed, down into the canyon made of water, or not. The magicians conferred in a tight circle, murmuring strange words, and igniting flash powder, and invoking evil spirits, and throwing some dust up into the air, to watch which way it blew, and how it fell as it scattered, and a couple of them muttered weird things as they cast lots in the sand. They kept at this for a few minutes, until the patience of the commander snapped, and he shouted at them to stop, and give him an answer.

The wizards gathered momentarily into a tight little circle again, and then their leader said, "We cannot tell."

The commander exploded, "What do you mean?"

The head wizard said, "The signs are confusing, and do not agree. It is confusion, and unclear."

The commander roared, "Useless fools! If you can't do better than that, grab swords, since you are going down there first!"

Right after that, the commander kept his word, and shaking wizards started down the slope into the strange water-walled canyon, trembling with each fearful step, eyes wide with terror. A couple of the less calm among them actually soiled themselves, but knew they had better stay shut up, and keep on walking, since the commander was not the man with which to argue. He answered directly to Pharaoh, and did not tolerate a "no" answer from anyone less.

The man chuckled, as he watched the not-so-brave wizards stumble downhill. "Okay, you first dozen charioteers, pick up those wimps, and let's get rolling!" The commander did not care a bit about the lives or well-being of the wizards, but he did not want to have to explain later to Pharaoh how he and his men had ridden them down under their chariot wheels.

One of the factors was, not only his fear of Pharaoh, and his contempt for the cowardly wizards, but his overall hatred of the Hebrews. He had never liked them, and when the first born of Egypt had died, supernaturally killed by God, on the night of the Passover, his own oldest son had died that night, too. Now, the only good Hebrew, to him, was a dead Hebrew. He did not sense the internal presence of the dragon, in his own heart, and mind, and he just thought that he personally hated Hebrews more than he loved his own life. No matter what, he was going to kill them all.

The enemy was there, driving the commander on, and with him were about a quarter of a million demons, all pushing the soldiers of Pharaoh into a murderous hatred of all things Hebrew, in an attempt to exterminate the nation of promise. If the devil could destroy Israel, then the Messiah could not arrive through Abraham, Isaac, and Jacob. The devil was still laboring under the false assumption that he actually was ever going to make God's Word become untrue. He never has, and he never will. He cannot beat God.

The enemy would not have had the guts to press the attack any further, if he had seen the mighty army in place, just waiting for him and his demons to get close enough, so that they could not make a run for it. Although the dragon still had the power to appear as an angel of light, all of the good, faithful cherubs, and all of the good angels, had perfect invisibility, and the blessing of the Most

High was upon them in battle, so that they could stand quietly ready, unseen, even by any of the evil spirits, including the dragon, as they waited eagerly, with drawn, flaming swords, that were still also kept invisible, until the perfect moment. They waited patiently, as the enemy, and its' demons, and all of the evil humans, began to enter fully into the giant water-canyon. As they rode, in chariots, or marched, they passed between the walls of seawater on each side, separated by over a mile, and the whole army, of about a quarter of a million men, and a quarter of a million demons, was so intent upon the hot pursuit, that they did not much take time to look into the walls of water, which they were passing between. If they had, they would have seen tropical fish, and large fish, of all kinds, including sharks, huge turtles, a type of octopus, or two, and maybe a huge Humboldt Squid, or two, which could be hungrier, and much deadlier, than a large white shark.

The strip of land upon which they were marching was a solid formation, like a suspension bridge, spanning the gap across the extraordinary depths of the Gulf of Aquba. To the south, the underwater terrain opened downwards into a huge, undersea chasm, similar in depth and grandeur to the Grand Canyon. To the north, another canyon existed, though not quite as deep, or long. Before the Flood, the northern canyon had been where everything began, and had been the sight of the original Garden of Eden, hemmed in on all sides by mountains. The mountains were still there, all around the sides of the Gulf of Aquba, except for a small, wide level place, called the Nueva Peninsula, which jutted out into the gulf, and led directly onto the ledge, which formed the upraised path, which now was being used as a dry road.

As the last of the Hebrews made it completely, safely across, and well clear, of the mysterious water-canyon, and, at the same time, the last of the army from Egypt had entered now completely inside the boundaries of the water-canyon, the good Lord decided that the moment was right. Suddenly, He opened the eyes of all of the enemy spirits, including the dragon, and all of his demons. As they saw instantly the vast Army of Heaven, standing there right in front of them, flaming swords drawn, and chariots drawn by horses of fire, with mighty war-angels, with hot fire-arrows, and burning spears, all sort of licking their chops in eagerness to hunt down everything evil, and kill, or bind it, fear seized every one of the enemy spirits, including the dragon. The good angels did not scare him, but the person using his unimaginably enormous hands to hold back the seawater was staring at him, right in the eye, and smiling a very frightening smile, with eyes that reminded the devil of the Eyes of Almighty God, that day in the Garden.

The dragon screamed, and turned away to try to flee, forgetting immediately all about the others that had followed him into battle. As soon as he did, he stopped short, seeing the cherub Michael standing there before him, sword drawn, and flaming like a supernova. Confusion set in. If that was Michael, just who was the one behind him?

As if in silent answer, the dragon felt fear escalate instantly into panic, as he felt the crushing, inescapable grip of the huge, white hands that had just been holding back the waters. As the cherub Eden-el tightened his deadly grip further, so the dragon could not even take a breath again, the worm gasped out, "But how? You're still on duty at the Tree of Life!"

As soon as the cherub Eden-el had moved his hands, the sea rushed back in, to where it had been trying to return, for hours, while he had held it open. The entire Egyptian army (and all of their rampaging chariot horses) was not able to survive the instant twin tidal waves that brought annihilation. The General of the angels, Tzedek-el, had brought over 700,000 war-angels with him this day, and they made short work of catching and binding that portion of the demons of hell, that had been at that battle. As the men of the Egyptian army were dying, the Lord had opened their eyes, to see just what kind of opposition that He had sent against them, so that they would understand, as they died, that they had attacked God!

As the cherub Eden-el held the dragon still, so the cherub Michael could come over and grab the worm, to drag the dragon back to the Mariana's Trench again, for a few more cold, dark years of forced introspection, the strongest cherub, the great Cherub of Energy, laughed, a great, booming laugh, that sounded like all of Heaven and Earth together were joining in the laughter. He said, "Yes, I am still on duty, at the Tree of Life, so that you and your kind cannot get to it. It is still right there where it was, deep under the water, miles to the north of here. It is not possible for it to die, whether under the ocean, or not. If God had planted it on the moon, the moon would have sprung forth oceans, and covered itself with lush green growth! You were just asking for it, when you got within reach of my hands, or came near my turf. I have been waiting to kill you, ever since you attacked my friends, King Adam, and Queen Eve. One day, the good Lord will give me the honor of binding you, and throwing you into the Fire, to die! Until then, stay away from me, or I will hurt you very much!"

As Eden-el finished, he gave the dragon an extra strong squeeze, and broke one of the thing's wings. As the dragon screamed in pain, Eden-el said, "Oh, shut up. You know that you will heal in a few days. I just want you to think carefully about this, if you ever think about coming this way, again!"

Michael took the thing out of the tight grip of his brother cherub, Eden-el, and smiled, as he dragged the now-silenced dragon away. Michael looked back, and said to his friend, "Okay, okay, he gets the point! Don't play too rough with him, yet. We don't want to anger our good Lord!"

CARDIOMA

Have you ever heard that word, or anything similar, before? Neither have I. Perhaps there is another way to correctly express something that could be described as a cancer of the heart, but I have never even heard of any such disease. Perhaps it exists, but is extremely rare.

The reason for this fact could be that the human body lives according to its' own wisdom, in certain things. We are, indeed, fearfully and wonderfully made. You cannot teach your body how to keep its' heart beating, while you sleep, and you cannot remember to breathe, once your awareness fades out. You cannot train your flesh to feel pain, or heat, or cold, or pressure. Also, you cannot micro-manage your own immune system, to send your little white blood cells, T-4 bacteria-phages, and other anti-bodies to concentrate their counter attack, here, or there, against invasion.

The body has been granted enough wisdom, by Almighty God, to know how to do all of these things, and many more, special things. It knows, without us telling it, when to shiver, and when to sweat. It also knows, that, at the top of the priority list, when it comes to defensive measures, there should always be listed first the things like brain, heart, lungs, and other priority survival functions, like core temperature. The body, and all of its' excellent defensive weapons, and systems, always keep a very close watch, on brain, heart, lungs, etc. Even though we hear of both brain cancer, and lung cancer, we do not seem to hear much about heart cancer. Perhaps, the body focuses its' strongest anti-cancer weapons against any possible attack against the heart, to prevent what would certainly prove fatal, before it can form. As if, maybe, the system considers such a disaster tantamount to death, itself. Indeed, when people do have heart attacks (though not from cancer), they often do not survive the attack. (That's usually because the heart is worn out, plugged up, or traumatized, too intensely.)

The Word of God warns us to keep our heart, with all diligence, since out of it are the issues of life. That is a true gem of wisdom, since what your heart is set upon, is what you think about, and what you desire, and what you strive to achieve, or posses, or experience. (Strong medicine, this watching what's truly down there inside your own heart, huh?) Do you want to know what is in your own heart? Look at the things in which you delight, the things for which you work, the things for which you plan, someday, and what you are trying to achieve with your life, and your strength, and your time, and your money. I am sure that you and I have this much, at least, in common: when I make my self take those long, deep stares into my own internal abyss, at the core center of me, I like some of the things which I see in there, and I sometimes dislike some of the things which I see in there. It shows me how, and how much, I have changed, for the better, over time, and it shows me how much more I still must change. The brightly-lit, ultra-sharp clarity, that the Lord Holy Spirit brings into my perceptions, will not allow me the self-deception of thinking that everything is always okay, in my thoughts, words, and deeds. Neither will He allow me to remain deceived by the enemy, in any form, but He shines a spiritual x-ray into the hidden things, and makes the mask of evil turn transparent, to reveal the monster, which is hidden, under a false-hearted person's plastic smile.

    Jesus gave us the ultimate litmus paper test: "by their fruits, you shall know them." This holds true for other people, and what their inner motives really are, but it also holds true for each of us, ourselves.

If a person's words and deeds match, then they exhibit integrity. The closer the match, the greater is the integrity. The fruit which a person bears, into the lives of others, is expressed, either as unselfish, and genuinely a gift of love, or else, self-interest-motivated (or, selfish) and not a gift at all, but an attempt to obtain a self-centered objective, or payoff.

The unselfish fruit is wholesome, nourishing, and good, for both the recipient, and the donor. It enhances life, and joy, and increases love.

The selfish "gift" is poisonous, destructive, and evil, for both the recipient, and the donor. It destroys life, and joy, and exterminates love.

So, there is indeed a type of cancer of the heart, and it is selfishness. It is rooted in pride, triggered by envy, and manifested by foolishness. The person whose heart is uncaring for the well-being of others, has chosen to set their love upon themselves, and lives a terribly lonely life, never trusting anyone, thinking everyone else is as corrupt inside as they are. The journey is miserable, with no escape, all the way down to a lonely grave.

Let us thank God, through Jesus Christ, that there is an escape hatch open for us! If we can trust Jesus, enough to confess our most horrible sins unto Him, and ask Him to forgive us, and to help us to change, and to become less evil, then He is faithful, and just, and He forgives us, and, as the Holy Spirit within us, changes us to walk in the pathways of righteousness, following Jesus home, like little tag-along brothers and sisters, of the King of Kings! There is a reason why He showed us His great power, and goodness, by healing people that no one else ever had been able to heal, before

Him. No one else, except Jesus, can ever heal that spiritual cancer of the heart, called selfishness.

He has begun to heal me, some. I am not quite as selfish as I used to be, once upon a time. Glory to God!

YOUR WAY

We know You have a plan,

And that we can trust You.

We know You know the things,

With which we're dealing, too.

We know You know our need.

 Please, meet it with God-speed.

Please, place within each heart,

The right things, from the start.

Please, weed out all the sin,

And put the right things in.

Whenever we might stray,

Return us to Your Way.

Help us to obey You,

All our lifetimes through.

GULF OF FIRE

The five men had cash. Not many people asked too many questions, if you paid them up front, in cash. It did not present a problem, when they wanted to rent an old fishing boat, to "go out over the weekend, and do a little fishing, and some beer drinking". The owner of the boat was glad to make the extra money, since fishing was still partly restricted, after the horrible oil leak from the broken well.

He showed them how all the vital parts of the vessel worked, and made quick photocopies (in his office, near the dock) of all their driver's licenses. Their names seemed normal enough, and he figured they were maybe college kids with some money, that did not want to spring for a luxury cruise. Their cover story was well thought out, and he watched them load a bunch of fishing gear, and some groceries, and several cases of beer, onto the boat. As he finished topping off the fuel tank, he warned them not to run out of fuel, and get stranded, since being towed in would cost a lot. He also warned them to keep the radio turned on, in case of emergency, and to wear life jackets, in case they got too drunk, and fell overboard.

As they loosed the lines, and moved slowly away from the dock, they all waved back at him, but did not seem particularly festive, considering what they had said they were going to do. He shrugged, as they faded smaller and smaller. He turned, and started to go back to his dockside office. For some reason, he stopped, just after he walked inside his door. Suddenly, on impulse, he grabbed his set of binoculars off of the desk, and ran back out to the dock. He searched for his boat, then found it, and adjusted the focus to clarity. As he watched, he saw two of them on the stern, throwing some things off of the boat. The boat was so far away, that it was impossible to make out any real details. Puzzled, he walked slowly back to his office, wondering what they were dumping. He had not left anything very valuable on the boat, so it must not be anything important. Still, it made him wonder.

It was not until he had a bad dream, about 3:00 A.M. that woke him up, in a cold sweat, with shaking hands, and a panic-struck mind, that he turned on his bed-stand lamp, and fumbled for the phone, and called one of his closest friends, the local sheriff. The man listened, grumpy, and sleepy, at first, but sat up immediately, asked a few more pointed questions, then thought a few seconds, thanked his friend, the boat owner, and then called some other people he knew, that had to be told about this, at once!

The men had headed the boat right out to sea, accelerating to all ahead full as soon as they cleared all the navigation buoys. They knew where they wanted to go, and it was not just a recreational fishing trip. They headed straight for the thickest part of the huge offshore area of the almost six thousand deep water oil rigs. They wanted to be as close as possible to the thickest concentration of offshore rigs they could find. With the modern internet, it had taken them less than two hours to find a chart of all the positions of the rigs, with a satellite shot of where all of them were anchored.

As they were steaming full speed toward what they estimated to be the approximate center of the thickest concentration of rigs, others were racing to intercept them, and the race was a close one. The men on the boat had been moving all afternoon, and into the night, staying the same determined course, and they had less than two hundred miles to go. The other boats, and the helicopters, and the jets, had further to go, but in those cases, were traveling very much faster, and the problem the interceptors had to overcome was that, to single out a particular fishing boat in the dark, a boat that resembled hundreds of other fishing boats out there, was not an easy task, especially since the men on board had had the sense to kill the radio, and run the boat with no lights. Radar in the interceptor boats and the aircraft could do a lot, but it was not all-seeing.

By this time, it was 4:00A.M. The hunt had been going for about thirty minutes. What had triggered the massive response was that the boat owner's dream had replayed the incident where he had seen the men dumping something off the stern. In his dream, suddenly his vision had seemed to zoom in, telephoto-lens style, and he clearly saw that what the men were dumping was the cases of beer. In his dream, this had seemed puzzling, and the next second, he seemed to hear them speaking in a foreign-sounding language.

Suddenly, they stopped talking, and looked silently in his direction, and then one of them began to raise his voice, in the call to prayer which is heard in Arab lands. That was what had shocked him back to waking, and forced the middle of the night panic call to his friend, the sheriff. Of course those guys would not need the beer, since they only had brought it along for a cover story. None of them drank any alcohol. It was against their religion.

After he had hung up, the boat owner had immediately gone to the fax machine, and then had sent his friend, the sheriff, all of the things which he had photocopied earlier that day. As soon as the sheriff had finished talking (quickly) with Homeland Security, he had forwarded the faxes to them. A few moments later, his phone rang again, and Homeland Security told him who the men were. The I.D. cards were all phony, but the photos were clear enough that the face-recognition computer programs found them in the database almost instantly. They were very bad people, indeed, and were among the top ten most wanted terrorists in the world. Oddly enough, they came from several different countries, including Iran, Yemen, Afghanistan, Chechnya, and even the Philippines. They were bound together only by a radical hatred of Israel, and, of course, the United States, which had helped Israel stay alive, many times. They had planned this for over a year, starting the day after the news about the oil leak had raced all around the world. They had seen a strategic advantage, and taken steps to use it.

What they wanted was to destroy the U.S. economy once, and for all, and they figured the total annihilation of all of the oil rigs in the Gulf of Mexico might just do it. What would normally have been impossible to accomplish, was now a very real possibility, since the entire Gulf was now a very dangerous blend of water, oil, and methane gas within the layers of water, which had replaced a lot of the oxygen in the water, and killed millions of sea creatures. The government had either been lying, again, or they had badly miscalculated the extreme levels of petrochemical molecules saturating the water, all over the Gulf. Either way, the terrorists had taken a calculated risk. Either it worked, or it didn't.

The trigger mechanism was, of course, a small nuclear device, often called a suitcase nuke. It had been easy to load it on the boat, right in front of the owner, concealed within their fishing gear, boxes, and bags. After they had left the shore far behind, they finished assembling the ignition device, as the beautiful sunset glowed orange. They weighted the device, since a surface detonation would not produce the desired effect. A special type of wire, such as the kind used in bathythermograph drops, was attached to the trigger, so it would be manually detonated by the crazy men in the boat. They were expecting to wake up with seventy two of their own personal virgins, once the trigger button was pushed.

Just about the time they thought they were near enough to the precise target area they wanted, they slowed the vessel, and turned on a light on the deck, to say a final round of their strange prayers (to the devil) and to drop the device over the side into the water. They were within a mile of several large offshore rigs, and the blast should easily take them out. That alone could achieve what they hoped.

As they were lowering the device into the water, a satellite hunting for them found them, aided by the small light they had turned on. After a quick zoom in, the orders were given, and fighter jets streaked toward them, missiles armed to kill. The men on the boat heard the scream of the jet engines, as they closed in, and the leader waited until the jets were very close.

Then, shouting something insane, about how great they thought an ancient moon-god demon was, the leader pushed the button! Seconds later, a strange, artificial sunrise lit the entire coastline of the Gulf States, from Texas to Florida.

The blast raised a column of water to the stratosphere, and the shock wave disintegrated the jets, and their just-launched missiles. The men, and the boat, were vaporized, as was a huge volume of the Ocean, and the resulting 1,000 degree plus temperatures ignited all of the petrochemicals saturating the Gulf waters. All of the rigs went up instantly, when the fireball, and the accompanying shockwave, as solid as a plate of battleship steel, slammed into them, at the rate of over 1,000 knots. A tidal wave hurled itself toward New Orleans.

Whatever Katrina had done, it had been nothing, compared to this.

About two hours before sunrise, a strange and terrible light was dawning all along the Gulf Coast. The fire started in the petrochemicals was racing at hundreds of knots toward Florida, spreading further and further. A huge column of steam and hot water vapor roared into the night sky, now brightly lit by the evil fire. Within a half hour, the entire northern section of the Gulf of Mexico was ablaze, and everything, and everyone, any where near the water was dying, or already dead. The poisonous smoke and vapors choked all into death immediately, if the fire did not get them. All of the Southern States died that night, and over a fourth of the United States was made uninhabitable, for hundreds of years.

The crazy devil-worshippers had succeeded, beyond their wildest dreams. This strike would severely cripple the

U.S. in a lot of ways, for a long time. Israel would be much more vulnerable, from now on, without their mighty big brothers, now no longer able to protect them.

There was one part of the demon-possessed fools' plan that did not go as they expected. Even though they had been vaporized so fast that they had not even felt the heat of their own deaths, now they suddenly found them selves trying to tread water for air, except that it was liquid fire, instead of water, and every breath seared the lungs to charcoal, whereupon they immediately healed again, just so they would have to take another burning breath, and feel the burn again, all over. The agony all over their skin was unimaginable, and the fire that they were stuck in was much hotter than the nuclear fire that they had started, but they could not die, not yet.

The good Lord Jesus Christ was just making sure that they did not get to die their own second deaths, not until they had "repaid the very last mite". Then, they would be released, into smoke and ashes, forever dead, and gone.

THE SANDAL STRAP

For many years now, he had waited alone, isolated from all humans, and their comings and goings. He had another mission, rather than to be involved in the daily lives of the people in the cities. He enjoyed being all alone with the Lord, and did not feel the need to make any new friends, or to seek to find a wife, or to start and raise a family.

The Lord had later greatly praised him, and said that among those born of men, there had never been anyone greater. He was filled with the Holy Spirit, even before he was born. When Mary (who was the mother of his second cousin, Jesus) had come to visit his own mother, Elizabeth, he had somehow known, in his yet-unborn heart, that his Lord had drawn near, and the not-quite-ready baby had jumped as hard as he could, struggling vainly to leave the womb of his mother, right then, and to go to join his Lord, and cousin.

After he was thirty years old, the Spirit of the Lord had driven him to the Jordan River, and told him to baptize all of the people of Israel there, preaching unto them a baptism of repentance, for the remission of sin. He obediently did this, even though it was a somewhat humiliating event, every time that he had to kneel down, and then to untie the sandal straps, of the person's shoes, and wash their dirty, smelly feet, using nothing but his own hands, which were usually lifted upward, instead, in prayer. It was not like the easier act, done instead, in later centuries, where someone, who actually was, indeed, a holy man, pushed someone else, a new believer, under water, and perhaps, sometimes, sought his own glory, instead of doing it the humble, sincere, original Way, which the Holy Spirit had instructed, through the example which we know that Jesus, Himself, later demonstrated, right before the Last Supper. God hates our acts of pride, and baptism is not supposed to include any sort of pride, or glory, for the one performing the baptism. It was, perhaps, intended to be an act of humble obedience, to God, and sincere love, for both, the one performing the baptism, and also, for the one receiving the baptism. ("For men to seek their own glory is not glory.")

For sustenance, he ate wild honey, which is loaded with protein, riboflavinoids, vitamins, and a whole host of other mysterious ingredients, which are almost supernaturally strong, in their nutritional value, and disease-fighting capabilities. In addition, he also ate locusts: nuts, not grasshoppers. To eat bugs is against the Law of God. The locust is a type of nut that grows in Israel, and is delicious, and, like the wild honey, is wonderfully strong, in all the right ways. Occasionally, he also had figs, and other fruit that he found, on the trees and bushes, as he wandered from campsite, to impromptu campsite, all over Judea. He wore camel hair, which is amazingly soft, if woven properly. He had a leather belt.

One day, the local Hebrew priests and scribes came out to the Jordan, to interrupt him in his baptisms, and to challenge him, about just who he thought he was, and why he dared to baptize people, when the official priests were not even thinking about doing that. For them, it would have been way too degrading, to stoop down, having removed their fancy, holy robes, and to have to kneel in the shallow water, and actually touch the filthy feet of the commoners. At that time in history, the Jewish priests considered themselves some sort of royalty, and put on many high and mighty airs, all of the time. Everything that John did was about honesty, sincerity, humility, and simple giving, of truth, and wisdom. That was so anti-establishment that the money-loving hypocrites could not endorse his actions, but they knew that they could not easily stop him, either, since there were always several hundred people coming to be baptized, and a crowd that large could not be easily overpowered, and the resulting uproar would have ended with all of the priests taken, forcibly, outside of the walls of Jerusalem, and then stoned by all of John's followers, which already numbered in the thousands. Even the monster, Herod, had heard of him, and would not readily mess with him, unless he wanted to take on the resulting rioting, that would follow.

Instead of getting drawn into a stupid, pointless debate with them, and trying to defend, or justify, his actions, he just told them, that okay, yes he was baptizing with water. Then, he told them something that shut them up, and left them scratching their heads, in confusion. He told them, "Among you stands the One,

Whom you do not know. I am not worthy to stoop down, and untie the strap of His sandal. Coming after me, He is preferred before me, because He already was, before I ever existed. I indeed baptize you with water, but He will baptize with the Holy Spirit!"

The priests left him alone, and went back into town. The people kept on coming to hear John's preaching, and to be baptized by him.

The next day, Jesus Christ came, unannounced, unto His second cousin, John, and asked him to perform the baptism for Him. John was stunned. "I have the need to be baptized by You, and are You coming to me?"

Jesus answered him, "Even so, for thus it is fitting for us to fulfill all righteousness." Then John permitted Him, and, as Jesus came to the edge of the shallows of the Jordan River, John knelt down in the water, and reached out with trembling hands, and fearfully, but determinedly, loosed the strap of the right sandal of Jesus, and removed it, and washed the foot, of his second cousin, and his Lord.

As they finished, and then stepped back, a couple of feet, on to the river bank, they both suddenly saw Heaven opened, and the Lord Holy Spirit, descending in glory, yet hidden from most eyes, resembling a Man, but with great wings, of living fire. He landed upon Jesus, and then, as they both watched, He was sort of absorbed, right into Jesus, and vanished from sight, within the Son of God. A great, deep voice boomed down from Heaven, "You are my Son, the Beloved. In You, I am greatly pleased!"

When the Voice sounded, all of the people there fell, like dead men, right to the ground, except for John, who managed to kneel, face down, to the ground, still trembling with excitement, and fear! Jesus, alone, still stood tall, looking right up into Heaven, straight into the unbearable Eyes of the Father. They smiled at each other, a real Father, and His real Son.

During the next three years, Jesus Christ increased, while John decreased. More and more people followed Jesus, and many of them were the same people that had previously followed John. John had graciously agreed to the shift, and indeed said that was precisely the Way, that God had planned for it to happen.

There came a time of doubt, for John, when he was locked up in prison, by Herod. After a while, hopeless, behind bars, even the mountainous faith of John was beginning to crumble. After all, if this cousin of his was really the Messiah, why were the Romans still alive, or Herod, for that matter, and why was he still locked in a dungeon? The true Son of god should have no problem re-arranging things, into a more favorable scenario for Israel.

John sent messengers unto Jesus, and they forwarded the question, from John, whether Jesus was the Coming One, or should they give up on Him, and look for another? While the messengers watched, for about an hour, Jesus Christ healed many people, of every sort of disease, and cast out all of the demons that were infesting them. Then He turned to the messengers from John, and commanded them to return to John, and bear witness, of the things which they had just witnessed Him perform. As they left, Jesus explained that John was the greatest man ever, second only to Himself. The simple, yet profound, explanation was that all men, who believed in Jesus, believed in Him through the initial witness, and testimony, of John. This also included the very first apostles, too.

A short time after that, John was murdered, in prison, by Herod. John died believing in Jesus Christ, and trusting Him, as his own, personal Savior. Jesus was saddened, at the news of the murder of his second cousin, and friend, and spent all night, praying with the Father, alone, as He wrestled with His Own issues of faith, during the storms of life and death that swirled around Him.

A while after that, it was the most special evening of the Holy Passover, the night of Thursday, just before the Feast of Passover, which was Friday night. Thursday night was when they had to kill the Passover Lamb, to prepare it for the Feast the next night. It took many hours of work, to clean, and roast it.

All of the main disciples were gathered together with Jesus, in the upper room. Jesus rose from the table, and laid aside His garments, and girded Himself with a towel, and went around the whole room, washing each of the disciples' feet, in turn.

When He came to wash Peter, Peter had objected, and said that Jesus would never wash his dirty feet. Jesus smiled at him, and told him that if He did not wash Peter's feet, then Peter would have no part, in Him.

Peter over-reacted, and became the world's first "immersionist", demanding that not only would Jesus wash his dirty feet, but that He would also have to wash all of him, from head, to toe. Jesus immediately corrected that notion, saying that Peter was clean, had no need to be washed all over again, but just his dirty feet. He made a point of stressing to them that they were already made clean, clean through the Word which He had spoken unto them. They were made clean, by His word, not by immersion.

As Jesus finished, and then washed His own hands, and sat back down, all of their eyes were fixed upon Him, as they waited to hear what lesson He wanted to teach them. After three years with Him, they knew very well that He only did things for a good reason, and that He would explain it to them. They were correct.

He said unto them, "Do you know what I have done?" "You call Me "Lord", and "Master", and you speak truth, for so I am. If I, then, your Lord, and Master, have washed your dirty feet, you are commanded to do likewise, unto one another!"

Two thousand years is a long time, and that is about how long ago He gave us that example, and made it a direct command, which we are to obey, if we are going to go around calling Him "Lord", and "Master". How dare we allow ourselves the conceit, to think, even for a second, that we should try to change His Holy commandments?

If any of you want someone, who loves Jesus Christ, to wash your feet, contact me. Even though I have spent many years of my life in disobedience unto Him, I will not finish my life, that way. Instead,

I will finish it, His Way: obediently, humbly, in loyalty, to Him!

PROPHECY OF THE GOLDEN EAGLE

Two years, and twelve days. That's two, of something great, and twelve, of something small. That makes a grand total of fourteen, but is very unique, in that special configuration. That's two, great, and twelve, not as great, and the pattern reappears over, and over, throughout time, in significant events, and their quantities, and timings.

The first similar thing, that struck me, is twelve lunar cycles per year, but only two major solar extremes, the summer solstice, and the winter solstice. The next pattern, however it developed, is twelve hours in the day, followed by twelve hours in the night. Each segment has twelve small things (the hours), and the whole day has two large components, day, and night. It is not correct to think, "Hold it, that's actually twenty four hours!" Each set, of twelve hours, is, quite literally, as different as day and night. It is incorrect, to try to lump them all together, in one pile. (Jesus, Himself, said, "Are there not twelve hours in the day?")

Another pattern, similar unto that, is the fourteen generations between Abraham and David, and then the fourteen generations between David, and the carrying away into Babylon. Yes, there passed another fourteen generations, between the carrying away into Babylon, and the Christ. Still, the primary two components, of the development of Israel, as a nation, and as a people, were (1) from Abraham, until David, and (2) from David, until the carrying away into Babylon. The total, of fourteen generations, is sort of tricky, to divide into twelve and two portions, and to see, clearly, the two great, and the twelve, not as great, also hidden within this pattern, until one realizes that out of every fourteen kings of Israel, only about two were ones that God called righteous, and around twelve were ones He considered to be bad kings.

Solomon also had decorations and adornments, of gold, all around the Holy Temple, which he had built for God, and they were grouped in clusters and strings of fourteen.

The most striking pattern, like that, is the twelve apostles, and Jesus Christ, twice. If one understands, that the entire Creation, and Reality, as we know it, or even as it really is, beyond how we know it, is all deliberately patterned, and designed, to be a perfect, tailor-made fit for Jesus Christ, then it is not a leap to see how all of reality will keep on some how repeating that pattern, again, and again. It is fascinating, to look for hidden manifestations of that same deeply-interwoven template.

It was on October 9th, 2008. It was about the sixth hour, or noon. The golden eagle flew right over my head, turning when directly over me, and headed eastward, toward New Jerusalem, to meet Jesus there, when He returns. Two ugly black, noisy birds were trying to harass him, but he sounded his call, once, just as he turned, right overhead. As I watched, fascinated, he snapped out a talon, the right one, and instantly killed one of the pests, releasing it in less than a second, and it fell, already dead, and motionless, from about two hundred feet up.

Today is October 21st, 2010. The time gap, since I saw that real world, real time event, (and watched it happen, right before my eyes, and right overhead) is precisely two years, and twelve days, and three hours, until that moment, which occurred today, at the ninth hour, or three in the afternoon, which is the hour of prayer. At that time, I was delivered from a terrible oppression, which has been upon me for this whole time, all the time, while I have been fighting to keep on writing these books. I did not think that I could fight on much longer. It is hard to write positive, God-glorifying poems and stories, no matter how much one loves Him, if one is experiencing so much stress and depression, that life seems to be much more pain and trouble, than it will ever be worth. It is only by the grace, and power, of the living God, that a person can produce anything good, when in the middle of a long, miserable war.

At any rate, believe whatever you wish. I know what I know. I am not saying that I am supposed to be the golden eagle, or that I will ever, in this lifetime, make it as far as Jerusalem. I do know this: as soon as the release from trouble was granted (so wonderfully!) unto me today, by a miraculous deliverance, performed, in His infinite mercy, as a special gift and blessing, for me, personally, by a loving, and powerful Heavenly Father, I immediately saw the vision/memory of the golden eagle again, in my mind, as clearly as if it had happened this same day. I again heard his cry of victory, as he flew, replayed, in my memory, too. I had forgotten all about that event, even though it is recorded in my first book, 'When Light Became A Man".

The end of the matter is this: now, my spirit feels, once again, just like the golden eagle, on his way eastward. My soul, also, wants to soar, and leave the remaining solo attacker far behind, as I climb, higher and faster, on mighty, restored wings of faith. I do not have time to be bogged down with foolishness, any longer. I have shown the Lord my faith, by my works, as He commanded. Now, bless His Holy Name, He has also shown me His faithfulness, by His miraculous works for me!

Now, please join us, brother and sister eagles. We, too, must be about our Father's business! We will all meet Him, soon, in New Jerusalem. That's where the eagles will be gathered together!

SIEGE MENTALITY

History has been altered. Volcanic eruptions, plagues, wars, tidal waves, major climate changes, the Great Flood, the opening, and closing, of the Red Sea, are some of the factors which have radically turned the path of human events. When the astronauts first beheld the Earth rising above the horizon of the moon, and took photographs of that event, it became instantly, absolutely certain that our home planet is a very small, lonely thing in the huge, black sky. Things, that change the course of human history, are monumental, because they affect the future of all intelligent (by definition of terms, only) physical life-forms in the whole universe. Also, there is, of course, only one God, and only one universe, despite what a psychotic scientist (so-called) did to a cat in a suitcase, a long time ago. (Confused people do not reach sane or valid conclusions. Their twisted views of reality warp their understanding into folly, and their comprehension, of the real truth, into nonsense and lies.)

One of the aspects of warfare that has been around from the earliest days is the siege. If someone can build a fortress, then, someone else, given enough time, troops, and maybe a special sort of equipment, such as siege towers, catapults, and so forth, can ultimately find a way to destroy the fortress, and then, the inhabitants.

Cities without walls did not last very long, in ancient times, as was also the case, with nations without armies. If you wanted to last more than a few years, you had better get a walled city, or ten walled cities, and enough fighting men to defend them all.

What could be the purpose of a siege, except greed, a poison fruit of covetousness? The people setting the siege are bent on owning what belongs to the people within the fortress, but the owners do not want to give it up, not without a fight.

The earliest known siege, if you wish to regard it as such, may be the Ark, under siege, for over a year, by the world-wide sea, all around it. The ocean had killed everything else, except for the fish, and so on, but the floating, wooden fortress of land-walking life forms endured the long siege, and kept the inhabitants safe, until the danger was gone. The outcome of that siege was of special significance, for the entire human race.

A type of one-man-siege was what the prophet Joseph endured, as he was in chains, or, at least, in prison, and it was an ancient, savage, Egyptian prison, at that. The outcome of that personal, one-man siege turned out to also be of key importance to the survival of the human race, during the later famine years. As with the Ark, God brought Joseph through the long, unimaginable ordeal, and the one-man fortress weathered the storm.

About four hundred years later, Almighty God, and His mighty warrior, Moses, set down a never before seen siege, against Egypt, and Pharaoh. The outcome of that siege was also of pivotal importance, to the future survival of the whole human race, as was anything that affected the survival of Israel. Otherwise, how would our Savior ever have arrived, as He did, in total fulfillment of all of the ancient prophecies about His arrival?

The next major use of siege warfare which we encounter is when Joshua and Caleb come to destroy Jericho. The Israelites did not want any of the possessions of the people of Jericho. As a matter of fact, they were exclusively forbidden, by God, to keep anything, at all, alive, or dead, that had been a part of Jericho. Only one Hebrew soldier was unwise enough to disobey that command, and he shortly there after paid, with the lives of himself, and his whole family. God had meant what He had commanded. The reason for the siege of Jericho was so that the Israelites could re-possess the land which God had promised unto Israel. All of the nations there, when Israel crossed the Jordan, were squatters, and permanent invaders, and usurpers, and thieves, of the land which God had guaranteed to reserve for His chosen nation, the People of the Book. Jericho had to go, as did the Jebusites, in Jerusalem, and other such deadly pests, which were infesting the Promised Land. They had to be exterminated, like other parasites.

There was a major siege which occurred during the centuries of the judges. Eleven of the tribes of Israel gathered against the tribe of Benjamin, which had holed up, in a fortress city, rather than turn over to justice, by extradition, men of their own tribe, which had done atrocities, and brutality, all the way to death, of a poor helpless girl, from Bethlehem, all during one long, hellish night. (She was found naked, and dead, on the doorstep the next morning.) The result of that siege was that only six hundred men (only men), from the tribe of Benjamin, survived the total annihilation that the other eleven tribes finally achieved, under direct orders, from God. It took centuries for the remnants of Benjamin to rebuild at all. Why was the outcome of that particular siege of pivotal weight to the future of all humans? Because, God was not about to tolerate such evil, in the midst of His chosen people, is the simple explanation. If He was going to be able, in future years, and centuries, to adequately bless them, so that they could grow into the mighty Israel of David, and Solomon, then they would have to be, at least, decent enough to not have that sort of poison in them, anywhere.

(Later down the road, Saul was the first king in Israel, and he was a promoted, used-donkey (like used-car) salesman. Is it surprising, that he was of the tribe of Benjamin? He later brought a ton of trouble to Israel, and tried, for thirteen years, to hunt down, and kill, David, all because of envy. He ended up disobeying a direct order from God, and, not long after, he was wounded in battle, and finished himself off, and that was the very same day that his son Jonathon was also killed, and his grandson was crippled, in an accident, that same day.)

We know that there were also two major history-changing sieges: first, the three year long ordeal, done by the Assyrian king, Shalmaneser. The result, at the end of that, was that Samaria fell, and all of the ten northern tribes were forcibly scattered to the four winds, unto the ends of the Earth.

There were also two sieges by the Syrians, under Ben-Hadad, but both of those were supernaturally defeated by God. One time, God blinded the eyes of the Syrian Army, until they were captured, disarmed, fed, watered, and sent home by Israel, but without their swords, or horses.

When the same Syrians came back again, a few years later, the good Lord had had enough. This time, he sent one mighty war-angel, the General, Tzedek-el, which then exterminated almost two hundred thousand enemy soldiers, in a short time. The outcomes, of those two sieges, also determined the survival of Israel, as a people.

The second major, history-altering siege was when the Babylonians overcame Israel, and carried everyone away. As when the Assyrians had proven unstoppable, in the time of Micah, the Babylonians altered the course, and standing, of Israel, from that time, even until 1948. Israel was never the same again, after that.

A strange variance on the theme then presents itself. When the grandson of Nebuchadnezzar was conquered, by the Medes and the Persians, a change for the better was granted unto Israel, since, not too long after, they were allowed to return to Israel's land, and to begin to try to rebuild their city walls. When that siege, of Babylon, was over, good things began to be possible, again.

Rome destroyed Jerusalem, again with the use of siege tactics, which resulted in the Diaspora of the Jews. This was certainly future-changing for Israel, since this began the times of the gentiles. This event started the final long countdown, until the return of Christ.

It is not certain just how much history was altered by the siege, also three years long, of Masada. Israel was already scattered, and being scattered further, all the time. The outcome was significant, in certain ways, however. Rome had committed untold money, time, and manpower to the task of over-running Masada, so they could make a terrible example, of the resistance movement fighters which were trapped there. When the Romans finally breached the fortress, all they had was a hollow victory, because of God's merciful release of the captives, into a gentle death, during the night. When the news made it around the ancient world, the concrete notion of Rome as impossible to defeat was shaken. A few decades later, in 211 A.D., Rome lost its' grip in England. About another century went by, and Rome began to start feeling a lot of heat from wild northern tribes, which were mounting a decades-long type of siege against Rome, itself. All the time, Rome did not realize that the real change was that the Holy Spirit had set Rome in siege, and He was conquering the pantheon-minded Romans, and making them start to believe in the only real God, the God of Israel. His assault did not come, with massive armies, but one person at a time, just the way that every one is granted salvation.

There have been several more pivotal sieges, such as Constantinople, now modern Istanbul. No doubt the outcome of that event turned world history into a certain direction.

The first Crusade, and all of the others, absolutely played their significant parts, also.

Modern equivalents, like the siege of Moscow, the Battle of Britain, and others, from World Wars, have been deciding factors in future world events, in profound ways. Now, such things affect the lives of even more people than in previous eras. Sieges never end in a draw. One side always loses.

Whether it is a personal siege, like with the prophet, Joseph, or a city, or a nation, it still happens, even in modern times. The most recent example that springs to memory is Sarajevo, during the Balkans' Wars. There is little doubt that siege tactics still are a favorite strategy, used with no hesitation, and little restraint. An enemy can be brutal, and heartless, even against his own countryman, as when the Yankee army attacked a defenseless Atlanta, with no army in range, to honorably have a chance to protect the civilians, which were old men, women, and children, and their puppy dogs, too. That was not enough cruelty. They also burned down the entire city. That was not the only desolation which was done by the North. Sherman heartlessly used a tactic, that was also a Nazi favorite, when he burned everything, including every building, and home, and every field growing food, in a sixty-mile-wide madness, over a hundred miles long, right through the heart of the breadbasket of the South, Georgia, which act, of monstrous cruelty, actually produced more destruction than a nuclear blast, minus the radiation poisoning. (The Yankee army had little concept of honor, or fair fighting, man to man. They struck at women, and children, as cowards often do.)

Perhaps you (like me) have spent a little time, sort of being under a type of siege, whether medical, financial, or whatever situation, or distress it could be. It is the thing which makes you feel like you are surrounded on all sides, and there is no escape visible. It is the thing which makes you fight, to get up, and to face another day of struggle, and sometimes you only do it because you are trying to actually be a person of genuine integrity, which performs the promises, which were made. (Words and deeds match, with God, and they should, also with us.)

The nation of Israel is also surrounded, on all sides, and people are trying to over-run it again, in its' modern manifestation, as a nation. There is not much reason to wonder why the men reading their Torahs, and worshipping during the Hebrew Feasts, and even walking around their own neighborhoods, and going to the grocery store, can often be seen carrying their Uzis, hanging in easy reach from a shoulder strap. If you were always surrounded, and had sneaky enemies with no regard for human life (losers which would rather kill women and children, than face real soldiers, one to one) all around you, then you would gladly carry a loaded machine-gun, all of the time, too. It's like a spare tire: you sure hope that you never need it, but you better have it, and know how to use it, anyway, just in case.

So, the outcome of any siege is never a draw. One side always loses. Do you remember how many times God delivered Israel from destruction? Neither do I, but it was a bunch. Why? Not for their sakes, but for His Holy Name's sake, and because of the oath which He promised to Abraham.

The only hope, sometimes, for outlasting a siege, especially when it has gone on a very long time (say a year, or three years, or fifteen hellish years) is that perhaps the good Lord will see fit, in His infinite goodness, and wisdom, to lift the siege. He can do it very suddenly, indeed, in a single night, by the sword of a single good angel. He has all kinds of interesting and surprising Ways to force a peaceful resolution, whether the enemy wants it, or not. He can even suddenly, with no warning, take a man straight out of a life-in-prison sentence, in ancient Egypt, and move him instantly into the royal palace, and place the reigns of power and authority in his just-released hands, that a short time before that, were still held fast in chains, and captivity. From the dungeon, to the second highest throne in the land, and it was the most powerful kingdom on Earth, at the time.

So, I do not know what choice others make, but as for me, and my house, either I can, and will, trust the good Lord Jesus, or there is no real hope for me, or any one else, whoever will not. If we had no one that really could save us, can you imagine the dismal, dark world which that would produce? I know that I would not want to live in it. Are you not glad, as am I, that we were born into a time, in world history, when Jesus has already been here, the first time? Now, we can eagerly anticipate His return, unto His Own home planet, which is here. At times, I still do wonder if He will cause the siege to lift, before He comes back, or not.

I guess it does not really matter, in the long run. What does matter is if we hear what He told us to do, and we live by it. We should do as He warned us, to obey, and to build our foundation on solid rock, or to disobey, and be swept away! He did say that storms and floods will come. He also said to cheer up, since He overcame the world!

TAKE AWAY THE STONE

The time had passed so quickly (whether having fun was any part of it, or not) that, before he realized it, almost four years had slipped by. The responsibilities that he had inherited were a bit different than those which his father had carried. His father had been Simon of Bethany, and he was exceedingly well known in all of Jerusalem. His dad had been one of the Sanhedrin, one of the seven ruling High Council members. Simon's specialty might have been called "Minister of Commerce", since he was the one that handled all trade negotiations, and agreements with other nations, and, in disputed cases, also ruled final decisions in local or national matters, which concerned fair trade practices.

Simon had also lived in Bethany, and had been, in official title, the Mayor.

Unofficially, he was the richest man in the town, which was a town of rather well-to-do folks, from Jerusalem, that would rather live about two miles away from the masses in the city, including the Roman soldiers that were stationed near downtown Jerusalem. Bethany was the ancient equivalent of the modern, upper-class suburban town, with a sort of country-estate concept to the large homes there. A more famous council member, named Joseph of Arimathea, was another man which preferred the country-estate type home, in another upper-class suburb, called, obviously, Arimathea.

The family wealth, and position, which saturated the lives of Lazarus and his two sisters, did not come as new things with them, either. One of his rich ancestors had even had a beggar, also, ironically, named Lazarus, which had waited outside the ancestor's gate, begging for crumbs, until he died. The story had been lost through the generations, since almost seven centuries had faded away its' traces. Only Jesus Christ remembered those actual, historical events, many centuries later, and He had told the story in a parable. All of His parables were true, actual events, which He selected to tell, as they, each one, perfectly fit the point which He was trying to communicate.

The whole thing had been coming for about two years, starting when his dad, Simon, had first become sick. Simon became known, as the months passed, as "Simon the Leper" instead of "Simon of Bethany". They were helpless to do anything to help, and the priests had not been able to obtain divine healing for Simon, no matter how much of his vast wealth he gave them. Finally, he was released to his rest, and his son and his two daughters buried him in a cave on the family land, which was a large spread, of many acres, outside of Bethany itself.

About two years ago, which had been about two years after Simon had died, Lazarus became 20. That is eight years older than Jewish Law declares manhood. At that time, he had heard of a strange new prophet, even more recent than John, a Man which could cure any disease, cast out demons, and work any miracle which He wanted. The curiosity grew, and became interest. The young man prayed about it for a while. One day, he told his sisters that he would return soon, and he went to find the Master.

After several days, and many inquiries, he managed to catch a glimpse of the prophet, and with Him, His dozen or so closest followers. They were heading out of the town, and he hurried to catch up with them. Long before He should have logically heard or noticed Lazarus, Jesus had stopped them all, to wait for him, as he drew near.

After a single question, about how to inherit eternal life, and a follow up question, about what measures were still required, to assure eternal life, the young Lazarus went away sorrowful, since Jesus had just told him to sell everything which belonged unto him, and give it all away to the poor people. Lazarus was extremely rich, and to give away everything was a very tall order, indeed.

Over the next year, or so, Lazarus could not forget the meeting with Jesus. Something very deep within the joy-filled eyes of the King of Kings had burned into his memory, and would not go away. His own thoughts kept echoing the Words of Jesus, and the sound of His voice was still crystal clear, in his mind. The very centermost heart of Lazarus began to change, and he started to think, well, why not? After all, it's not as if I do not have enough money for a thousand people. Why not give some of it away?

From that time forward, the focus of Lazarus began to lock more intently upon Jesus, and His teachings, and he began to become fully convinced that this Jesus fellow really was the Son of God, maybe. He discussed his ideas with many of his young friends, which came over to visit often, and that opened the chance for his sister, Martha, to run around playing hostess. She was still single, at 19, and was ready to snare a young husband, and some of her brother's friends were cute, and well-off, too. She overheard the things they were discussing, as she brought drinks, and snacks, and fixed meals for them. Martha had been kind of forced to learn to play hostess early, after their mom had passed away five years ago. Her younger sister Mary was extraordinarily sweet, but they had all had to help raise her, after the loss of their mom. Martha was sort of a rich-girl socialite, too, as was her sister, Mary, as was normal in a family with as much wealth and power as they had accrued through the centuries. These days, Martha, and Mary, would have been debutantes, and big brother Lazarus would have been the rich playboy in town. Martha had grown into the vacuum left by her mom's absence. Now, she acted like a kind of mom to both Lazarus, and Mary, and also resembled a woman named Martha Stewart, (not to be born for another twenty centuries) in the way in which every single silverware arrangement had to be set just perfectly.

Younger sister Mary had run into trouble, after their father had passed. She was sad, and angry, and kind of unhappy with God, for taking away both their mom and dad. She smarted off, sometimes, to the old ladies at the synagogue, and made scowling faces at even the High Priests! If she had not been the daughter of their former partner, Simon, and the little sister of Lazarus, one of their biggest financial supporters, they probably would have tried to set her up, to catch her in a sin, or maybe some blasphemy, if they could trick her into one, in front of two witnesses. After that, they could have stoned her. That was one of the favorite ways the council had devised to remove a troublesome adversary, permanently. It had worked many times. These days, they had to do a better job of framing the victim, since they had to convince the Romans to perform the executions, as Rome had forbidden the Jews to kill anyone, even guilty criminals. It was too much trouble to silence her smart mouth, yet.

The Master came through Bethany again, and this time, He visited Lazarus, personally, and spoke about the Kingdom of God, unto all those from Bethany, and also many from Jerusalem, which were friends of Lazarus, and came to see and hear. As He spoke, Martha served dinner and refreshments to the huge crowd of people, with the help of over a dozen of their household servants. She noticed, with irritation, that Mary was sitting right in front of Jesus, about six feet away from Him, staring as though in a trance, and listening, like a tape recorder, to everything that Jesus said.

As she brought a full cup of water over to hand Jesus, He paused a moment, at the end of a portion of His message. He turned, looked at her, smiled, and said, "Thank you, Martha," and then, He had taken a sip of water. As He did this, Martha, instantly said, not, "You're welcome," but, "Lord, make my sister get up, and help me serve all of our guests!"

Jesus corrected her, gently, but firmly, and continued His lesson.

There were many other places, to which He had to go, and it was a long time before He made it back around there, again. This time, He came in response to the sad news that Lazarus had suddenly become ill, and had then perished. As He approached the town, one of the townspeople, living on the edge of town, recognized Him, and ran to tell Martha and Mary of His arrival. The boy saw Martha, told her, and left. Martha ran out, discreetly, and followed the neighbor boy back to meet Jesus, as He approached. After they spoke a moment, He promised her that her brother would live again, and asked her if she believed that He was the Savior, which would raise all men for judgment, one day.

Martha showed, right then, just how much her own faith had matured, since their first meeting, when she said, "Yes, Lord, I believe that You are the Christ, the Son of God!"

This confession of faith reveals how her priority had been re-focused, straight onto Jesus, instead of the circumstances, and how, even in her terrible sadness, and deep grief, she still trusted in Jesus, as the Son of God, and knew that He could handle anything, and that He would help them to do the same. This knowledge was something given unto her by the Father, as had been the case, when Peter had confessed, "You are the Christ, the Son of the Living God!"

Then, as He drew near the town, Mary heard from Martha, which had run back to tell her, that the Lord had arrived, and wanted to see her. They both ran out, as did a large group of the local religious leaders (some were there to genuinely show support for the remaining two daughters, of their former associate, Simon, and some were there, because of financial motives, including a few of the men which saw an opportunity to try to begin marriage pursuits, of either of the young women, since that was a lot of money, and property, of which they had just become the sole owners).

After the brief greeting between Jesus and Mary, He told them to lead Him to the tomb. This tomb was almost identical to the one which would become His Own tomb, less than two weeks from now. Rich men, like Joseph of Arimathea, and Lazarus of Bethany, could afford to have a cave, either already available for a tomb, somewhere on their property, or, they could afford to hire enough muscle to carve one out of the rock, when the time came. They all stopped, and marveled to see Jesus actually weep real, manly tears of grief for his friend. Jesus knew that Lazarus was better off, already graduated from this life, than to have to return to this sinful world, again. He also knew their excellent reunion would be a dramatic, but short-lived one, until after His Own resurrection. Also, He knew that this event would make Lazarus, as well as Himself, a hunted, hated man, to the High Priests. He wished that Lazarus could just continue his quiet rest. It made Him sad, to have to disturb his friend's peace.

    They all watched, expectantly, as He looked at the tomb, and wiped away the last trace of His tears from His eyes, with the back of His hand. He took a deep breath, and, looking up to Heaven, raised

His hands up, and said, "Father, I thank You that You have heard Me. I know that You always hear Me, but I said this because of these people standing here, so that they may believe that You sent Me!"

Then, He lowered His arms, pointed at the stone which sealed the tomb, and said, "Take away the stone!"

Martha, always aware of proper decorum, muttered discreetly to Jesus that there would be a stink, since Lazarus had been dead for four days. Jesus looked her deep in the eyes, smiled very slightly, and asked, 'Did I not tell you, that if you would believe, you would see the power of God?"

Then, He turned to the tomb, as the men finished moving the stone away from the entrance to the cave, and then, He commanded, in a strong, clear voice, but not a shout, "Lazarus, come forth!"

For a few seconds, nothing happened, as the people all held their breaths, and their hearts raced in excitement, and fear. They all had goose bumps.

Suddenly, a rustling sound, of cloth being dragged across dirt, and clumps of spices, and dry flowers, came from the cave. Seconds later, everyone gasped for breath, at the same moment, as they actually saw a dead man walking out of his own grave! Everyone, except Jesus, dropped face down into a curled up little ball of fear, praising God, in terror, instantly realizing the hidden, overwhelming power, revealed, that was buried deep within this human-looking carpenter.

After a few more seconds, Jesus commanded them, "Untie him, and let him go." (The hands had been tied in a position over the abdomen, to keep them in a restful looking pose, and the feet had been tied together, to keep them from spreading much, from rigor mortis. The two coins placed upon his closed eyes had kept them from opening, and then had fallen off, when he stood up, from the burial shelf. The burial shroud was a loose fit, and was not really tied on to him, but just draped over him. The thing, which was actually tied into a knot, was a sort of neckerchief, except that it was tied like they tie a rag for a toothache, with a folded neckerchief under the chin, and over the top of the front of the head. The resulting image makes the person look like they have a set of bunny rabbit ears, coming out of the top of their head, while the rest of the cloth forms a solid chinstrap.)

Many of the people who witnessed this miracle instantly believed, and followed Jesus, from then on. Astonishingly enough, there were some folks that personally saw, and heard, this unparalleled miracle, and were so crazy that they actually went away to plot (with the other chief priests) about ways to capture Jesus, and frame Him, so that they could kill Him.

Jesus had told the ironically appropriate parable about Lazarus (the beggar) and the rich man, and at the conclusion, the last lines of the parable, prophetically, are, "If they will not hear Moses, and the prophets, neither will they be persuaded, though one rose from the dead!"

There were fools there that day, which proved Him correct. There were the same fools, and others, ever since, which have continued to prove Him right, also, about the matter of His Own resurrection!

CURRENTS OF JUSTICE

It had not happened over night. The thing had been building, and gathering momentum, and growing more massive, and more toxic, and it was on the move, and it was moving their direction.

Three years earlier, Halliburton and British Petroleum had lied their ways into a disaster, and killed a major percentage of the food chain in the Gulf of Mexico. The damage had not been easy to see at first, except for the tiny fraction of tar balls, which arrived soon, upon some southern beaches, and a large bit of sludge, that ruined some wetlands.

The British were not concerned about the harm which they caused. The damage they were trying to limit was the loss of their public image. That image was revealed to be a plastic mask, fabricated from lies, and held in place by secrecy. Behind it was the real face of a monster.

That was not the only ugly thing working destruction in those events. There were traitorous elements at work from the American side of the Atlantic, also. Halliburton was certainly to blame, as was every person which supported or endorsed that company of evil, in any way at all. The mainstay of their support was always the Federal people, which sunk in huge amounts of time, and favorable voting, to give all sorts of unfair advantage to Halliburton, when it came to huge tax breaks, and the backroom-deal awarding of many special, extraordinarily lucrative government contracts to Halliburton, even if some of them were called "Black Water". Money was the master, for almost all of those wretches. Bad enough, that they had chosen a dead-end highway for themselves. Far worse, they dragged a whole lot of decent, God-fearing American citizens along behind them, spending millions on advertising, public relations campaigns, and a general propaganda blitz, which was designed to cover their guilty tracks, and keep their questionable fortunes rolling in. As long as their financial bottom line was always increasing, they never stopped to think about how bankrupt their souls had become. Since they judged others, and even their own lives, by how much money they had, the idol which they served, instead of God, was money. They feared personal poverty more than they feared the Judgment of God! They chose the approval of men, instead of the approval of God. They ignored the fact, that, that which is highly esteemed by the world, is considered abomination, in the sight of God.

The northern segment of the population of the United States never really chose to honor the Appomattox Treaty. During the Civil War, the Yankee army committed numerous war-crimes, against both southern soldiers, and also unarmed civilians. The reason why the Civil War is considered to be the first modern war is not that the weapons were made in factories, or that the movements of troops and supplies were accomplished for the first time, in such a massive way, by the use of locomotives and trains.

No, it was the intense cruelty perpetrated upon the South by their so-called countrymen. (If you are not aware of these facts, it is because our northern neighbors do not want the great-grandsons of the South to remember the truth. Check into your history books a bit deeper, and also, if you will do a little background, in-depth research, and you will find the same ugly truth.) Immediately after the war, the abuse and neglect continued, with the invasion of the carpetbaggers, and the scallywags. (When Jay Leno talks about something "going sour" he always uses the insulting term "gone south" instead. Fine with us, he can stay in his wrong-thinking attitude, way up there in Massachusetts, or out there in L.A.)

Even though slavery was clearly wrong, the justification used by Lincoln, so that his guilty conscience would let him sleep, and even more, so he could justify the brutal orders which he gave to his generals, was that it was a religious duty to destroy the South, and even warfare against unarmed civilians, and undefended cities, was therefore sanctioned as okay. The Civil War was never fought about slavery. Lincoln promised the Southern States that he would never abolish slavery. He made that false promise right after he had snuck into Washington, in the middle of the night, so he could survive for long enough to make his inauguration lies. When he signed the Emancipation Proclamation, he did not give a darn about blacks. Instead, Lincoln had done it in the hope that the news would cause the slaves to revolt, and help the northern army, which was getting its' butt kicked very badly right then. (A few months before that, Southern troops had set the White House on fire. They almost succeeded, in trying to burn it down.) Open racism was very present and visible in the North, not only in the South. For example, the northern army generals expressed severe doubts about the courage of the Buffalo soldiers, (black men, enlisted in the Union army) and said they would run, when faced with real battle. Of course, that was a lie.

This general systemic anti-Southern bias never quite died. It was passed down from one Yankee generation, to their descendants, all the way into modern times. When Katrina hit, the northern government turned its' back on other Americans, and betrayed them, just because they lived in the South. At the time, the Yankees were wasting billions of dollars, and a lot of American blood, in a city half a world away. They wanted to keep the crude oil flowing, even if it meant spilling some American blood to do it. That was the yard stick by which they measured: billions for Baghdad, but only a few million for New Orleans.

The same Holy God Almighty which had watched the bondage of the blacks, and used the horrible war to liberate them (thus showing His goodness, and power, by bringing good out of evil), was also watching the long decades of anti-Southern bias, and also saw the hypocrisy of the Yankees, which cared not a thing about the slaves.

The pride had been crushed out of the hearts of the Southerners, forever. That was done by God, to set things straight. It did not automatically grant the Yankees a free hand, to become even worse jerks after the end of the war.

When the Macondo well poisoned the Gulf, it set the stage for a final settlement in the ongoing case. When the crazy fellows had detonated the nuke in the depths of the Gulf, and ignited all of the flammable molecules which were spread all through it, the resulting cataclysm had destroyed all remaining life, in the waters of the gulf, and along the shoreline, for over a hundred miles inland. Again, the northern-biased government said a lot of great sounding promises about helping the surviving southerners. What they actually did, which was no surprise, was, once more, turn their collective backs on the South. The devastated people of the South were left alone, again, to fend for themselves, against disaster. The Yankees actually blocked other nations trying to bring help, declaring the whole Gulf to be a hazard, and patrolling with U.S. Navy vessels, to keep it sealed up, like a tomb.

All the while, the ocean currents were not listening to Washington, or London, and were only responding to the Voice of God. Over the next months, the poison waters began to be driven up along the entire East Coast, killing and ruining everything along the way. Within a year, Washington, New York, Boston, and every other coastal city, was then destroyed by the deadly waters. All marine life near the shore died. Birds died. People died. Cities died. States died. And, many years after the abuses done by the North had started, (by means of taxation without representation, all the way back to 1820, which caused the Missouri Compromise) the result of their own evil was returning upon them.

London was not yet ruined by the wet death. It took it longer to cross the whole Atlantic. It did eventually arrive, months later, carried express by the Gulf Stream current. Before very long, the owners of British Petroleum and all of their British cronies and investors were watching the destruction of their own land, even though they had thought themselves to be so remote, as to be immune to consequences for their deeds.

Both the Yankees and the British forgot the fact that Almighty God enforces justice, even if He sometimes takes a while to do it. They also forgot that His Memory is flawless, and permanent, and His Arm never grew short, and He never grew weak! God said that vengeance is His, and that He will recompense. We should all fear Him, indeed. Even as He executes judgment, He does it with an ironic sense of humor. "Black Water" seems quite appropriate, in this case.

HOW TO DECLARE SPIRITUAL BANKRUPTCY

Sometimes in life, people experience things which cause change. If a person loses a job, it might be difficult to continue in the same house, or even the same neighborhood, or the same state. If a person has a serious injury, or illness, or a long-term disability, it may be impossible for things to remain as they were.

This can cause a double whammy effect upon the person, when they are already trying to cope with the increased difficulty, or additional pain, or reduced income. It can increase until the person is no longer able to endure the stress or despair. Suicide should only be used in rare circumstances, as when faced with a certain, unavoidable alternative, which would literally be worse than death, such as with those people which were trapped upon Masada.

There are other alternatives to end the stress. Liquidation of assets may be a necessary step. Acknowledgement of all debts, and honestly seeking honorable means to resolve the matters, are absolutely required. Strict adherence to humble truth is demanded, if the issue is to be properly resolved.

The individual, or corporation, which has found its' self in serious trouble, has to present the information, accurately reported, with no omissions, and no deceit. This presentation must be accomplished in due process of law, and must be guided by a certified attorney. This information, by means of the attorney, is presented unto the judge, to obtain the best possible resolution, and most beneficial outcome.

The judge must weigh the elements in the individual case, and render a just decision, to end all present disputes, and prevent future conflicts. The object is to help the person in need to become functional once again, by means of a second chance. Hopefully, the application of mercy, adhering to justice, will enable the person to rebuild properly, being, as expected, a little older, but very much wiser. The bankruptcy law is there to help people in need, not to finish destroying them.

In our financial and legal system, there are some good laws, and some which are not as good. The general concept is that things be done honestly, and honorably, with fair outcome given to all. Once the process has been worked through, a fresh start is granted, and new hope returns.

A different set of conditions is present within the spiritual realm, however. All of the Laws of God are always good, without exception. Whereas the laws (legalities) of men may be possible to obey, almost totally (if you think you obey all of the legal guidelines, when was the last time you drove even one mile per hour over the speed limit?) for most people, in most cases, it is not humanly possible, in this fallen world, to obey the Law of God, and never sin. There was only one Man which ever did that, and we ended up hanging Him on a wooden cross, for telling us the truth, that we are all sinners!

Even if a person is dimly aware that they owe some money to somebody, they are not precisely sure just how much, or to just whom, until they get the bill. After that, if they can pay it, they usually will. Most people really would rather pay all of their bills, on time, if they could.

A parallel exists when the Lord Holy Spirit convicts a person's heart of their own personal sin. Once the Holy Spirit opens their eyes, so they see their own sin, they immediately see how wrong, and broken, and incomplete, and useless to the Kingdom of Heaven, that they actually are. This revelation causes fear, self-loathing, misery, and a sincere desire to change, into something less disgusting. Often the person will, for a time, struggle to actually change, which will result in failure, after failure. Eventually, the person either will become discouraged, and give up, or seek extra help, from the good Lord, to actually change, or, more accurately, be changed.

For those which persevere until this point, there is now help. When the person is able to finally get down upon their knees before God, and humbly, sincerely agree to let God run things His Own Way, instead of trying to always cut a deal, or make a trade, or work out some compromise, then actual change has already begun. The sincere humility was the required, but still missing, element. Now, the person is ready, at last, to see and hear things the Way which God says to see and hear them. Now, the reconstruction can get started, since the fortress of stubborn pride stood right in the middle of the construction zone, and it had to come down, first. Many of the things which we suffer are allowed just with the single purpose of knocking down that nearly-invincible tower of pride which we each build within our hearts. Once it is out of the way, God can do things His Way. Then He can prove, once more, as always, that His Way is best!

So, once you know all of the debt, and honestly admit it, you still need an attorney. Please allow me to introduce you to your very own personal defense specialist. His Name is Jesus Christ! There is no finer defense available, and no additional defense is needed. Trust Him, ask Him, thank Him, and obey Him, and follow Him. Stay with Him all the Way home. If you commit your life to the good Lord, He can, and will, cover your greatest debts, and set you free, to choose to follow Him.

You see, there is a strange aspect to all of this. Yes, in both types of case, debts can be resolved, honorably, and a new future can be granted. In the case of Jesus, your defense attorney is also your Judge, since the Father has committed all judgment to the Son. Get things straight with Jesus, and from then on, learn what He said to do, and do it, and keep on doing it. If you stick with that program, and never quit doing it, you will not carry any debt, at all, the day in which your own personal account is opened for judgment.

If you stumble along the Way, get back up, and get going again! A football player does not quit the game every time he gets tackled. Neither should we. Just be honest about your mistakes, and stay patient about your need. When you do not understand, then trust, instead!

WOLVES BEYOND THE GARDEN

As Adam and Wolf were approaching the edge of the clearing, next to the great tree house where they lived, they heard a sharp yelp, of pain. They were startled, and after a split second look at each other, they flashed into a streak of motion, skidding to a halt as they came into sight of Eve and She-wolf. Eve was looking, in stunned surprise, at her left arm, where there were a few tooth marks, and some drops of red blood dripping out of them, slowly. Her jaw was slack with disbelief. As she heard Adam and Wolf come running up, she turned, looked at Adam, then pointed at She-wolf, and said, "That wolf-bitch bit me!"

As soon as she said that, all three of the others, Adam, Wolf, and She-wolf, turned sharply, and stared in shock at her. Eve had always been the sweetest, most kindly speaking person they knew. To hear her speak with such vicious animosity was bizarre, especially since it was aimed at her beloved huge puppy, She-wolf. The only thing more odd than that was the obvious physical change in Eve, because her beautiful wings were missing, leaving behind only two small bumps, which were fading into her shoulder blades more every minute. In addition to that, no one had ever seen a human bleed before that moment. No human had ever been vulnerable to injury or pain, before earlier that hour. Now, somehow, due to the interference of the worm, Eve could be hurt, and bleed, and she had lost her wings, and she could exhibit real anger, and unjust hatred.

Adam asked her, "What happened?"

She replied, "Well, I was trying to start fixing dinner, since I figured you were hungry, and I was, too. I was trying to hurry up, since I thought it would not take you long to kick the enemy out of here. She-wolf kept on thinking it was time to play, and kept jumping up wanting snacks, until finally, I yelled at her, and gave her a big shove, to make her let me work. I guess she thought I was rough housing with her, because she snapped at my arm, and it hurt! Then it started to bleed." As Eve finished telling him, she began to shake, and cry. Adam was very confused, and, like billions of men since him, tried to do what he could to comfort his distraught wife. It was the first time he had ever seen her cry, and it sort of freaked him out. (What the heck was wrong with her today, anyway? And where on Earth were her beautiful wings?)

She-wolf came slinking over, hesitantly wagging her tail, but very concerned about her momma. Of all the people, or other creatures, which might be on the hit list for She-wolf, Eve would never be one of them. She-wolf loved Eve, and would gladly give her life for

Eve's, just like Wolf would do for Adam. This was a family built on love, and trust, and it grieved She-wolf, to the center of her heart, to have injured Eve.

As Adam dried her tears, Eve said, "It's all right, Baby. I know you did not mean to hurt me. I'm sorry I called you a bitch!"

Wolf muttered something under his breath, and quietly chuckled to himself, at his own joke. Adam replayed the comment his furry buddy had made, intensifying the volume level in his memory, and he clearly heard Wolf say, "Actually, she really is a bitch!" and then heard his throaty chuckle again, too. Adam glanced at Wolf, and the two met eyes, and Adam smiled ever so slightly, just because it actually was pretty funny, and then shook his head a bit, to warn Wolf not to make any more jokes, right now.

Adam bandaged her wounds, and fed them all supper, and made sure that She-wolf knew that she was a much treasured member of the family, as always. Adam fell asleep, at last, with his mind racing, full of unanswered questions. He knew that the good Lord would come by to chat with him for a while, in the morning, since it would be the Day of Rest, and the Lord always came to meet with him, every seventh day, that way. The questions would have to wait, until the morning, when he could get some real answers.

After a restless night, full of weird and disturbing dream-fragments (nothing clear, or concrete, just unsettling things), Adam woke up early, to see that Eve was already up, and he heard her downstairs, at the base of the tree house, fixing them breakfast. She did not have pots and pans to clatter, but she still managed to produce a whirl of activity, with the simple utensils which she had.

After he had rubbed his tired eyes, and stretched a few times, he climbed down to see what she had ready. He was exceedingly hungry, this morning. Also, he had to get moving. He had his regular appointment with the Lord this morning, in their usual place in the Garden. It was a few miles away, and he and the Lord had been meeting there every seventh day for centuries, long before God made Eve. Adam always went there alone, since it seemed wrong to include any other person at all, even his beloved wife, when it came to meeting the Lord, Face-to-face, in that special, holy place. It was, and always would be, a private, personal time for the two of them to talk, and share deep thoughts together.

As he arrived at ground level, he turned to see Eve, and the things she had set out for their breakfast. Adam had been given the privilege and responsibility to name all the creatures, which he did. (The first time he saw Eve, he said, "Whoa, man!" and the name has stuck, to this very day.) The right to name all of the trees, plants, and flowers had been reserved for Eve, and she had named each of them, with attention to the secret meaning of the plant's name, which described its' properties. He knew she had a special gift for combining just the right blend of plants, nuts, berries, and so on, that would produce a delicious meal, every time, and the strength which it would yield was always good, too.

As he glanced at her, he instantly noticed that she had wrapped some large leaves from some of the plants around her torso. In later centuries, people would have described her outfit as a sort of one-piece swimsuit thing, but made of large leaves. He was puzzled. As she motioned for him to come and sit down at the table, she smiled, and asked, "Do you like it?"

"No."

In later centuries, men would have to learn the hard way, every man for himself, the painful lesson which was granted, for the first time in history, free of charge, to Adam, as Eve exploded in anger, accusing him of everything, except being a good husband!

Shocked, Adam stood up, went straight over to her, lifted her up, easily, by her arms, as he gently (but firmly) held her at eye level, and quietly asked, "Woman, what is going on with you?" If Adam had already sinned, he could have felt fear, and his voice would have been shaking with it. After she calmed down a bit, he went on to say, "You know I always loved the way you look, which is perfect, and absolutely beautiful, just the way that Father made you. Why would I like your trying to hide it from me?"

After a few more reassurances, they sat down to eat. Adam said thanks, and then began to dig in, since he was really very hungry, this morning. He noticed a strange new fruit on the plate, which was unknown to him, although there was something vaguely familiar about it. As he picked it up, and sniffed of it, it made his nostrils tingle, and, oddly, raised the hackles on the back of his neck. It smelled delicious, but he was suddenly very suspicious of it. Out of his peripheral vision, he noticed that Eve was watching his every move intensely, but silently. As he glanced her way, he noticed in a flash that her knuckles were white, where she was gripping the edges of the table, ultra hard. There were lines of stress, and deep nervousness, woven into her beautiful features. It somehow made his skin crawl. He put the thing back on the plate, and stood up, ready to walk away, to go meet the Lord, for morning worship.

Eve also jumped up from the table, and skipped around to his side, and threw her strong arms around his neck, and whispered in his ear, her breath hot, her eyes wild, and a sly smile on her face. "I know what you like. All right, I'll forget about wearing clothes again, from now on, and we can stop and do those strange things you like so much, any time you want, as often as you want. Just try a taste of this new fruit for me, okay, Baby?"

Adam, like billions of men after him, was unwise enough to make a fatal mistake, and listen to his wife, instead of God. Still, he did at least ask, "That's not that special tree that God told us to leave alone, is it?"

Eve, instead of answering his question, picked up a slice of the fruit, and smiled at him, handed it to him, and undid her leaf-wrapping, instantly distracting his mind, the same way her daughters have been doing ever since.

Adam was so busy, staring at her, and memorizing every detail, as he had for many years, that he put the slice of fruit into his mouth, without paying it much attention. It seemed unimportant, at the moment, but it was the most foolish choice in history. The fruit tasted very sweet, at first, but, within a few seconds, began to turn sour, and then extremely bitter, until he spit out every trace of it, but still could not be free of the bitter after taste. He began to gag, and hack, until he finally had spit out enough, so that he could catch his breath again. As he wiped the traces of tears, from the hacking, out of his eyes, he looked up, and saw Eve, and immediately shouted, "Woman, what's the matter with you? Cover yourself! Put those leaf things back on, right now! Make me some of them, too. Hurry, God's coming this way, and He will be here soon!" As he said that, Adam felt a thing down inside his heart that he had never felt before. He was afraid. Maybe God really would kill them, for disobeying Him. After all, that's what He said He would do, and Adam knew from centuries alone with God, that God never lied.

For the next several minutes, they both scrambled frantically to fabricate and install the world's first wardrobe upon themselves. Just as they were finishing the final tying of the vines around everything, to hold it all in place, they heard a deep, powerful Voice behind them.

"Adam."

As soon as they heard it, they both dropped instantly to the ground, and covered their faces in fear. Both Wolf and She-wolf did the same thing, hiding their eyes under their paws.

The Voice went on, "You missed our meeting, for the first time. Why?" God did not ask because He did not know. He wanted Adam to admit the sin, so God could forgive it. Without honest confession, there could be no forgiveness granted. To have done that would not have been justice.

"I heard you coming, and I hid, because I was naked, and afraid."

"Who told you that you were naked?"

After a few seconds of silence, God asked, "Did you eat of the tree which I commanded you to stay away from?"

Adam instantly sold out his wife, and said, "The woman, which You gave me, gave me the fruit, and I did eat."

The Lord looked at Eve, and said, 'What's your version?"

Eve replied, "The serpent gave me the fruit, and told me we would not die if we ate it, but that it would make us smart, like You."

God shook His head, and said, as He handed them buckskin outfits, instantly produced by miracle, and tough leather boots as well, "The worm will pay. War is already raging in Heaven, because of it. You are already dead, although you do not yet know it. Because you each have honestly confessed your sin, and I can see genuine remorse and repentance deep in your hearts, I will forgive you, and resurrect you to life, because of your descendant, My only Begotten Son,

Jesus, since He will someday pay your sin debt, in full. You will still have to pass through death, and after that, you must sit in silence beside My Throne, and watch with Me, all through the history of the world, as your children fight and lose against sin, pain, and death. You will know, the whole time, that you are the two people responsible for it all. You will have to wait until it is all over, praying all the time for it to stop."

God suddenly was joined by the most powerful cherub, the cherub of energy, Eden-el. God looked at him, and said, "Escort these two to the outer gate, and lock it behind them. No one gets in, or out, until the seventh trumpet!"

As the humans turned to follow obediently behind Eden-el, as he led them toward the gate, a voice called out, "Wait!"

It was Wolf. He stood up, and trotted, hesitantly, over to where God stood, in His blinding glory. Summoning every scrap of his very great courage, and it took all of it, Wolf said, "If it's all right with you, Lord, could I please go with them?"

God looked down at Wolf, and smiled, and said, "This is not a fun hunting trip, or exploration. You would not enjoy this journey."

Wolf nodded his enormous head, and smiled a Wolf-type smile, and said, "Yes, Sir, I know. It will be ugly, miserable, painful, and pointlessly insane, at times."

God smiled at Wolf again. "Do you still want to go, then?"

"Yes, Sir!" After a second, Wolf added, "Adam may need me to help him, in case the enemy tries to bother him any more. Also, I have to teach him how to hunt, and track, and work in teams with other men. He already knows how to howl at the moon with me!"

The good Lord laughed, as She-wolf also came up beside Wolf, silently declaring her own determination to go, too. The Lord smiled at them both, and said, "All right, then, you must know that once you leave the Garden, only the humans will still have the power of speech, but they will have to talk with words, instead of the mental picture language we all use now. Also, you will eventually die, as will all things beyond the gate. And, you could be hurt, or injured, or suffer great pain and sorrow, out there in the world."

Wolf, and also She-wolf, both nodded, and said in unison, "We know, Lord. We still want to go with them. They will need us."

The Lord chuckled, and said, "Very well. When all things are over, I will Personally reward you, and all of your children, with great, eternal honors, for your great love and loyalty, for My children. You will always be known as God's Puppies!"

With that, the wolves bounced up, tails wagging, and fell in beside Adam and

Eve, ready to go face a world full of hell with them. Before they could even take two steps, a gray flash appeared, and a hoarse, rasping voice said, "You're not going to leave me behind!"

They all turned, and saw that it was the little gray donkey. As they stopped, and waited for him to catch up, and She-donkey appeared also with him, they trotted to catch up, and fall in beside the humans. Donkey looked up at Adam, and said, "You might need someone to help carry things for you, if they are too heavy to lift."

They heard the Voice of the Lord, as He walked, invisibly, beside them, on the way to the outer gate. "Very well, Donkey! For your great loyalty, one of your sons will carry My Son into battle one day, in Jerusalem, and again, at the final battle, when We reclaim the Earth!"

They had almost reached the gate, when they heard a whinny, and a snort, from a great, thundering beast, which raised a cloud of dust, as he skidded to a halt beside them. He snorted again, shook his mighty mane, and looked Adam in the eye, and then looked at Wolf, and laughed a loud, high spirited horse whinny of a laugh. "So, you think that you can outrun me, just by sneaking away out of the Garden, instead of coming to play with us today, and chase around the fields, as we all love to do?"

Adam and Wolf looked at Horse, and Adam said, "This is not a game, today, friend Horse. We are being expelled from the Garden."

Again, Horse laughed his musical laugh, and said, "I know, King Adam! I still think you might need a fast, tough ride into battle, or if you have a need to cross a great distance, in a short time. Donkey is wonderful, but I can outrun him."

At this comment, Donkey brayed out loud, and then joined Horse in a good-natured laugh.

Adam looked over his own shoulder, and saw where his own wings were now missing, also. "Yes, thank you, Horse, and each of you, as well. Your help will often likely be the difference between life and death, for us. I do not ask any of you to come with us, but I do thank each of you, and bless your whole line of descendants, forever."

As they walked through the outer gate, and passed beyond Eden-el, the cherub began to swing his enormous sword, moving it in flashing arcs, which covered every possible angle of attack, from anything, or any creature, which might try to enter the Garden. The sword was moving so fast, it became a shining blur, seeming to fill all of the air space around the giant cherub. Even a machine gun could not have squeezed a bullet through, edgewise. The cherub of energy had unlimited strength, so, he could keep on moving that deadly blade at that speed and power, for eternity, if God wanted him to do it. That would be fine with him, too, no matter what God wanted him to do.

As the humans, and the six animals that had dedicated their lives to help them, sadly walked away from the gate into the Garden, Eve began to sob quietly, as the enormity of all the trouble she had caused came fully into her awareness. She stopped, and sat down in a heap, right on the ground. Adam kneeled down, and comforted her, mighty arms of love wrapped securely around her, as he assured her that God would fix it all, given enough time. She could not seem to calm down, until She-wolf came over to her, and nuzzled her cheek, with her cold, wet nose, and then, when Eve lifted her tear-streaked face just a bit, She-wolf began licking away her tears. After a few seconds of this, Eve could not help herself, and began to laugh a little, as they all came close to help calm her down, and tell her that they forgave her. A short time later, they all got up, and got moving again, looking for a good place to make camp, before sundown.

As He watched them walk away, God's heart was filled with sadness. Just because He already knew what would happen, before it happened, it was still a disappointment, anyway. The humans no longer could see into the spirit realm directly, so they did not see that God had sent over 100,000 angels to walk beside them, and also, although Eden-el was on assignment, and could not leave his post, the cherub Michael was walking with them, too. The devil was not going to be allowed to do any further damage unto this little family, at least not until years had passed, and Cain went crazy, and brought yet more sorrow. That was years away, though, and it was enough to handle, for now.

ABOUT THE AUTHOR'S LOBO

The whole thing began when two of my friends, Miguel, and Omar, which are both animal control Officers here in Farmers Branch, rang my doorbell, and told me, "We think we found a dog for you!"

This event had been their helpful response to a request on my part a couple of months earlier. Some evil raccoons from the creek had been invading my backyard, and had killed some of my pet cats. Since I am not supposed to use a 30-06 in the city, I needed a big dog, to stop them.

They told me he was a large shepherd mix. I told them I was going to name him Lobo, (since my last big shepherd had been named Lowen) and as soon as they heard me say "Lobo", they looked at each other, surprised, and then grinned at me, and Miguel said, "That's already his name!"

Well, as it turned out, I adopted Lobo, for ten dollars, and he has been one of the finest gifts that the good Lord has ever shared with me. He is appropriately named. He is seventy-five percent Alaskan wolf, twenty-five percent shepherd, and 100% wonderful! When they test the storm sirens, we go out in the backyard and have a great family-howl together.

Lobo helped me keep encouraged, as I struggled to finish these books. He kept me out of despair, when times were tough. He kept me looking, to find the positive, good things to write about. As far as his original intended job description, there has been only one raccoon here since he arrived. That is, only one that did not make it back over the fence in time. Most of all, he showed me God's love.

BACK-JACKET TEXT

In the very beginning, the King wrote out the entire, complete Book, and locked it closed, with a seal that only He, and no one else, could ever open. In the pages of the Book, He had written everything that would ever occur in Time, and also the names of every one that would be with Him in the world yet to come.

One of the Cherubs went insane (self-deceived by pride) and launched a futile attack against the King. The weapon was a lie about the Truth of the Book. The enemy never realized the truth, that even his own rebellion had been foreseen.

At the end of Time, the War will be ended, by the King, and those rescued from death will dwell with Him forever. Those who helped the enemy to fight against the King, and His Book, will be exterminated, forever. The War will be ended, but the King, and His Book, will remain, forever.